REAR ADMIRAL

HENRY GALLANT

H. Peter Alesso

THE HENRY GALLANT SAGA

Midshipman Henry Gallant in Space © 2013
Lieutenant Henry Gallant © 2014
Henry Gallant and the *Warrior* © 2015
Commander Gallant © 2016
Captain Henry Gallant © 2019
Commodore Henry Gallant © 2020
Henry Gallant and the Great Ship © 2020
Rear Admiral Henry Gallant © 2021

Other Novels

Captain Hawkins © 2016
Dark Genius © 2017
Youngblood © 2018

REAR ADMIRAL HENRY GALLANT

H. Peter Alesso
hpeteralesso.com

© 2021 H. Peter Alesso

This is a work of fiction. All characters,
dialog, and events
portrayed in this book are fictional,
and any resemblance
to real people or incidents
is purely coincidental.

All rights reserved.

No part of this publication may
be reproduced, stored in
a retrieval system, or transmitted
in any form or by any
means without prior permission
in writing from

VSL Publications
Pleasanton, CA 94566

ISBN-13: 9798755752350
Edition 1.00

∞

The hope has always been
for the next generation to be better.

United Planets —

1ˢᵗ (Home) Fleet
Fleet Admiral Simone L. Graves

> 4 Spacecraft Carriers –
>> *Arc Royal, Eagle, Hermes, Lexington*
>
> 4 Dreadnoughts –
>> *Conqueror, Colossus, Defiant, Superb*
>
> 4 Battlecruisers –
>> *Achilles, Agamemnon, Arduous, Audacious*
>
> 24 Cruisers
> 48 Destroyers
> 2 Stealth Reconnaissance Scouts –
>> *Cheshire, Siren*
>
> 72 Auxiliary Support Ships

Task Force 34
Captain Henry Gallant

> 2 Spacecraft Carriers & Starfighter Space Wings
>> UPSS *Constellation* CVS-647
>>> 36 Viper I – Squadron 6 - Lieutenant Glen Holman
>>> 48 Viper II – Squadron 8 - Lieutenant Lorelei Steward
>>> 6 Hawkeye – Squadron 10 - Lieutenant Kelsey Mitchell
>>
>> UPSS *Courageous* CVS-648
>>> 36 Viper I – Squadron 7
>>> 48 Viper II – Squadron 9
>>> 6 Hawkeye – Squadron 11

2 Battlecruisers – *Indefatigable* -
Captain Donahue
Invincible -
Captain Hernandez
12 Cruisers
48 Destroyers
2 Stealth Reconnaissance Scouts –
Warrior, Invidia
12 Auxiliary Support Ship

Task force 47 returns from the Dog Star, Sirius.
CVS-642 *Yorktown*

Marines
Major James Steward
1st Marine Raider Battalion

Titan —Battle Fleet
Admiral Vvorn
6 Spacecraft Carriers –
Vespa Class carriers 1-6
Starfighter Space Wing
256 Fighters
256 Bombers
48 Search
6 Dreadnought
6 Battlecruisers
136 Cruisers
288 Destroyers
188 Troop Transports

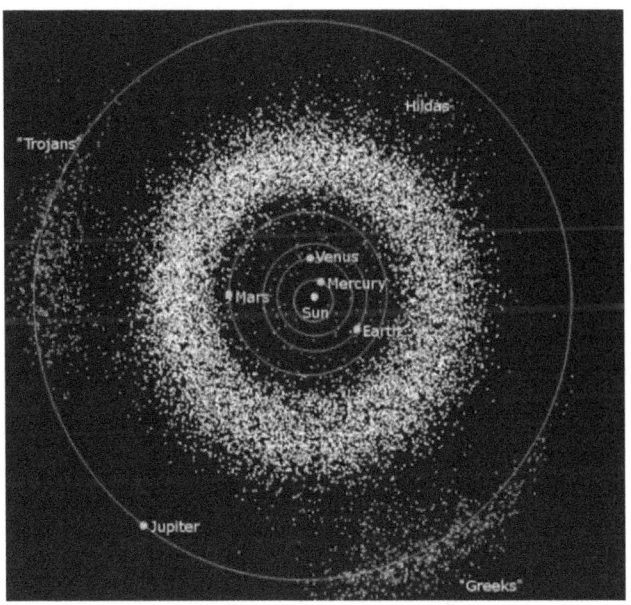

Radius of Solar System = $144 * 10^9$ km

Speed of Light 300,000 km/sec = $1.08 * 10^9$ km/hr.

= $25.92 * 10^9$ km/day

Light travels from the sun to earth in 8 minutes.
The perihelion for Uranus is 4.5 light-hours.

CONTENTS

Chapter 1 Far Away
Chapter 2 Very Close
Chapter 3 Launch, Launch, Launch
Chapter 4 Fools Rush In
Chapter 5 Last Rites
Chapter 6 Scapegoat
Chapter 7 Magical
Chapter 8 Recon
Chapter 9 Saturn falls
Chapter 10 Without Reflection
Chapter 11 Sortie
Chapter 12 Promotion
Chapter 13 Defeat is an Orphan
Chapter 14 Doors
Chapter 15 Cat and Mouse
Chapter 16 Nowhere
Chapter 17 The Right Stuff
Chapter 18 Full of Promise
Chapter 19 The Noose Tightens
Chapter 20 Without Dissent
Chapter 21 Faded Photograph
Chapter 22 War Paint
Chapter 23 Gambit
Chapter 24 Queen Sacrifice
Chapter 25 No Man Left Behind
Chapter 26 Checkmate
Chapter 27 Avalanche

Chapter 28 Superman
FROM THE AUTHOR

CHAPTER 1

Far Away

Captain Henry Gallant was still far away, but he could already make out the bright blue dot of Earth floating in the black velvet ocean of space.

His day was flat and dreary. Since entering the solar system, he had been unable to sleep. Instead, he found himself wandering around the bridge like a marble rattling in a jar. His mind had seemingly abandoned his body to meander on its own, leaving his empty shell to limp through his routine. He hoped tomorrow would bring something better.

I'll be home soon, he thought.

A welcoming image of Alaina flashed into his mind, but it was instantly shattered by the memory of their last bitter argument. The quarrel had occurred the day he was deployed to the Ross star system and had haunted him throughout the mission. Now that incident loomed like a glaring threat to his homecoming.

As he stared at the main viewscreen of the *Constellation,* he listened to the bridge crew's chatter.

"The sensor sweep is clear, sir," reported an operator.

Gallant was tempted to put a finger to his lips and hiss, "shh," so he could resume his brooding silence. But that would be unfair to his crew. They were as exhausted and drained from the long demanding deployment as he was. They deserved better.

He plopped down into his command chair and said, "Coffee."

The auto-server delivered a steaming cup to the armrest portal. After a few gulps, the coffee woke him from his zombie state. He checked the condition of his ship on a viewscreen.

The *Constellation* was among the largest machines ever built by human beings. She was the queen of the task force, and her crew appreciated her sheer size and strength. She carried them through space with breathtaking majesty, possessing power and might and stealth that established her as the quintessential pride of human ingenuity. They knew every centimeter of her from the forward viewport to the aft exhaust port. Her dull grey titanium hull didn't glitter or sparkle, but every craggy plate on her exterior was tingling with lethal purpose. She could fly conventionally at a blistering three-tenths the speed of light between planets. And between stars, she warped at faster than the speed of light. Even now, returning from the Ross star system with her depleted starfighters, battle damage, and exhausted crew, she could face any enemy by spitting out starfighters, missiles, lasers, and plasma death.

After a moment, he switched the readout to scan the other ships in the task force. Without taking special notice, he considered the material state of one ship after another. Several were in a sorrowful dysfunctional condition, begging for a dockyard's attention. He congratulated himself for having prepared a detailed refit schedule for when they reached the Moon's shipyards. He hoped it would speed along the repair process.

Earth's moon would offer the beleaguered Task Force 34, the rest and restoration it deserved after its grueling operation. The Moon was the main hub of the United Planets' fleet activities. The Luna bases were the most elaborate of all the space facilities in the Solar System. They performed ship overhauls and refits, as well as hundreds of new constructions. Luna's main military base was named Armstrong Luna and was the home port of the 1st Fleet, fondly called the Home Fleet.

Captain Julie Ann McCall caught Gallant's eye as she rushed from the Combat Information Center onto the bridge. There was a troubled look on her face.

Is she anxious to get home too?

Was there someone special waiting for her? Or would she, once more, disappear into the recesses of the Solar Intelligence Agency?

After all these years, she's still a mystery to me.

McCall approached him and leaned close to his

face.

In a hushed throaty voice, she whispered, "Captain, we've received an action message. You must read it immediately."

Her tight self-control usually obscured her emotions, but now something extraordinary appeared in her translucent blue eyes—fear!

He placed his thumb over his command console ID recognition pad. A few swipes over the screen, and he saw the latest action message icon flashing red. He tapped the symbol, and it opened.

> TOP SECRET: ULTRA - WAR WARNING
> Date-time stamp: 06.11.2176.12:00
> Authentication code: Alpha-Gamma 1916
>
> > To: All Solar System Commands
> > From: Solar Intelligence Agency
> > Subject: War Warning
> > Diplomatic peace negotiations with the Titans have broken down.
> > Repeat:
> > Diplomatic peace negotiations with the Titans have broken down.
> > What this portends is unknown, but all commands are to be
> > > on the highest alert in anticipation of the resumption of hostilities.
> >
> > Russell Rissa
> > Director SIA
> > TOP SECRET: ULTRA - WAR WARNING

He reread the terse communication.

As if emerging from a cocoon, Gallant brushed off his preoccupation over his forthcoming liberty. He considered the possibilities. Last month, he sent the sample Halo detection devices to Earth. He hoped that the SIA had analyzed the technology and distributed it to the fleet, though knowing government bureaucracy, he guessed that effort would need his prodding before the technology came into widespread use. Still, there should be time before it becomes urgent. The SIA had predicted that the Titans would need at least two years to rebuild their forces before they could become a threat again. Could he rely on that?

Even though he was getting closer to Earth with every passing second, the light from the inner planets was several days old. Something could have already transpired. There was one immutable lesson in war: never underestimate your opponent.

A shiver ran down his spine.

This is bad. Very bad!

Gone was the malaise that had haunted him earlier. Now, he emerged as a disciplined military strategist, intent on facing a major new challenge.

Looking expectantly, he examined McCall's face for an assessment.

Shaking her head, she hesitated. "The picture is incomplete. I have little to offer."

Gallant needed her to be completely open and honest with him, but he was unsure how to win that kind of support.

He rubbed his chin and spoke softly, "I'd like to tell you a story about a relationship I've had with a trusted colleague. And I'd like you to pretend that you were that colleague."

McCall furrowed her brow, but a curious gleam grew in her eyes.

He said, "I've known this colleague long enough to know her character even though she has been secretive about her personal life and loyalties."

McCall inhaled and visibly relaxed as she exhaled. Her eyes focused their sharp acumen on Gallant.

"She is bright enough to be helpful and wise enough not to be demanding," continued Gallant. "She has offered insights into critical issues and made informed suggestions that have influenced me. She is astute and might know me better than I know myself because of the tests she has conducted. When I've strayed into the sensitive topic of genetic engineering, she has soothed my bumpy relationship with politicians."

He hesitated. Then added, "Yet, she has responsibilities and professional constraints on her candidness. She might be reluctant to speak openly on sensitive issues, particularly to me."

McCall's face was a blank mask, revealing no trace of her inner response to his enticing words.

He said, "If you can relate to this, I want you to consider that we are at a perilous moment. It is essential that you speak frankly to me about any insights you might have about this situation."

She swallowed and took a step closer to Gallant. Their faces were mere centimeters apart.

"Very well," she said. "The Chameleon are a spent force. After the loss of their last Great Ship, they are defenseless. They agreed to an unconditional surrender. They might even beg for our help from the Titans. Their moral system is like ours and should not be a concern in any forthcoming action. However, the Titans have an amoral empathy with other species."

He gave an encouraging nod.

She added, "Despite the defeat of Admiral Zzey's fleet in Ross, the Titans remain a considerable threat. They opened peace negotiations ostensibly to seek a treaty with a neutral zone between our two empires. But we can't trust them. They are too aggressive and self-interested to keep any peace for long. One option they might try is to eliminate the Chameleon while they have the opportunity. Another is to rebuild their fleet for a future strike against us. However, the most alarming possibility would be an immediate attack against us with everything they currently have. They might even leave their home world exposed. But that would only make sense if they could achieve an immediate and overwhelming strategic victory."

Gallant grimaced as he absorbed her analysis.

She concluded, "This dramatic rejection of diplomacy can only mean that they are ready to reignite the war—with a vengeance. They will strike us with swift and ruthless abandon."

Gallant turned his gaze toward the bright blue dot—still far away.

CHAPTER 2

Very Close

With each passing hour, the *Constellation* was two million kilometers closer to Earth, but Gallant could not formulate a plan of action without more information. When they entered the solar system, the light from Earth was over two days old and everything appeared normal. He hoped nothing had happened in the intervening time to change that.

Gallant envied those lucky enough to believe that they controlled their own destiny. Those souls found life no more complicated than following their usual work and relationships routine. He never subscribed to that folly. Yes, he would strive, make choices, get prepared, and so on, but eventually, reality would step in with its elaborate random probability game—turning his future over to providence. Remarkably, in matters of career and love, he often displayed an eerie sense of timing. His career had been favored with more surprising lucky twists than not. But his love life had been fraught with unfortunate moments, occurring either too early or too late.

Now racing toward Earth, he found the future of both his career and love life in extreme peril, and his sense of helplessness was appalling.

He scanned the Earth sensor data, desperate to glean every possible clue from the photons streaming his way. But even in this moment of crisis, there were mundane distracting annoyances that demanded his attention.

Heat and humidity formed beads of sweat that rolled over a lock of hair on Gallant's forehead, distracting him from the emerging war crisis. He was reminded of the dilapidated condition of his ship.

Damn environmental system.

Several of the ship's oxygen generators, CO_2 scrubbers, and backup electric generators, required to maintain the atmosphere within the ship, were offline. With the environmental system malfunctioning, the air was choked with oil and grease from machinery operations. Little puffs of smoke appeared from the AC vents. If this kept up, there would be serious electronic casualties.

Like everyone aboard ship, he had always taken the air for granted, but like many critical ship systems a refit was sorely needed.

He asked pointedly, "Chief, when will I get my air conditioning system back?"

Chief Howard turned his pouty face away and made a fuss about checking the monitor equipment and twisted several dials. "Looks like it's going to take a while longer, Captain. The engineer is replacing the AI regulator. You know how finicky they are."

Like a scruffy, unkempt scarecrow, Chief Howard adjusted his poor posture and made a hangdog face. His appearance was a stark departure from his past fastidious habit of keeping his uniform in pristine condition. But alas, the deployment had not spared his wardrobe. His melancholy helped to make him an object of some amusement to the bridge crew, who despite these alterations, worshiped him. Somehow, he wound up on the *Constellation*, which was good for the United Planets. His simple Missouri upbringing helped make him the man he was. And despite his best efforts to be on good behavior, he couldn't help raising a chuckle from the crew whenever he hummed a distracting down-home country song during the watch.

Gallant wiped the sweat from his brow and turned his attention back to the war crisis when the sensor operator reported, "I'm getting an ambiguous signal, sir."

Chief Howard asked, "Well, do you or don't you have a target?"

The sensor operator said, "Somethings there I tell ya, Chief. I just can't get it in focus. It must be very stealthy and very far away."

The OOD, Lieutenant Clay reported, "Sir, we've intercepted a high priority sighting report from the *Cheshire*, a stealth picket ship monitoring Earth."

At 0940, Gallant read:

> From: *Cheshire,* picket station 003
> To: *Superb*
>
> Strange anomaly sighted two light-hours from the Moon base, bearing 093, mark 2.
>
> We are unable to distinguish the target clearly.
>
> It is on course toward Earth."
>
> *Captain Charles Jaeger*

Gallant turned to McCall and said, "Unfortunately, your analysis may prove correct. I'll bet that's a Titan fleet using the Chameleon stealth technology. It seems that the *Cheshire* doesn't have one of the halo detectors we sent from Ross. They would have seen through the Chameleon stealth technology at a fair distance."

She said, "Yes. That technology was the key to our defeating both the Great Ship and the Titan Battle Fleet at Ross. But Admiral Graves may not have distributed the devices we sent to Earth. He may have given them to SIA for further evaluation before manufacturing and sending them to our sentry ships."

Clay reported, "Another message from the *Cheshire*, sir."

At 0950: Gallant read:

> From: *Cheshire*
> To: *Superb*
>
> Request permission to investigate the

anomaly.
Captain Charles Jaeger

Clay added, "Sir, Superb replied. Their message read: 'No. We'll send a Hawkeye.'"

Gallant guessed how the *Cheshire's* orders might be worded: "Maintain sentry duty at assigned post and report all targets to fleet command. You are directed to assess the extent of any threat and observe and report the enemy movements and composition. At the onset of any hostilities, you are to maintain contact with the enemy for as long as possible and provide updates."

These circumstances didn't quite fit with the *Cheshire* captain's options. He would have to improvise and show a degree of personal initiative. It was a life-defining moment that appeared with a swift blinding emotion. What do you do? It takes uncommon sense to make a sensible decision. Everything would depend on this captain's audacity.

Gallant smiled when he heard that the captain of the *Cheshire* did NOT follow his orders. Instead, the captain sent the message,

At 1050, Gallant read:

> From: *Cheshire*
> To: *Superb*
> On my own discretion, I am proceeding to investigate the anomaly.
> *Captain Charles Jaeger*

Gallant grinned.

I like this officer.

Chief Howard said, "I know the captain of the *Cheshire*. He's Charles Jaeger, a regular Missourian Midwesterner. He still has a little of the wild west in him—stubborn as a mule. He'll poke that anomaly."

Soon the Clay reported, "Message from the *Cheshire*, sir."

At 1152, Gallant read:

> From: *Cheshire*
> To: *Superb*
> > Target has no IFF signal.
> > It is not a friendly.
> > Suspect it may be an enemy formation.
> > Recommend Earth go on high alert.
> > *Captain Charles Jaeger*

Clay said, "Captain, *Superb* responded, "Are you declaring this a bonified Titan target? Verify that you have a legitimate target."

The crew of the *Constellation* remained tense, waiting for more news. They couldn't see anything except one vague distant contact. All they could do was imagine what had happened from the scant fragments of late arriving radio communication. They were like an audience listening to a delayed broadcast of an old-time radio drama.

Once again, the OOD reported, "Message from the *Cheshire*, sir."

At 1202, Gallant read a message that had been sent in the clear.

> From: *Cheshire*
> To: *Superb*
> Contact! Contact! Contact!
> *Captain Charles Jaeger*

Chief Howard practically jumped out of his chair and shouted, "Good job, Charlie!"

There was a great stir of excitement on the bridge of the *Constellation*.

"McCall asked Gallant, "How do you think the Home Fleet responded when it got this timely warning?"

Gallant said, "If Admiral Collingsworth was still in command, he wouldn't have hesitated. He would have immediately ordered all ships to sortie on high alert. But I'm afraid Graves is not cut from the same cloth. He would wait for more information. He might have dilly dallied, hemmed and hawed, and responded with the least measure. This might not end well."

The next minutes dragged on relentlessly. Then, at 1217, Gallant read another message from the *Cheshire* that had been sent in the clear.

"The target is an enemy fleet. It is now very close."

CHAPTER 3

Launch, Launch, Launch

Space grew menacing. It began with a solar flare, blowing across the inner planets, strangely bright for this time of year. But even before it reached the *Constellation*, Gallant was aware that something ominous was approaching.

A fresh rush of disturbing information from the *Cheshire* declared, "We are under attack by hostile forces. This is not a drill. This war has turned hot again, and we need help."

In the span of time it takes a man to gulp down his coffee, Gallant was running into CIC to scan the screens showing the enemy targets.

McCall appeared at his side and said, "It's as we feared."

Then she brought up the database screens with SIA top-secret reports.

"Here is the SIA assessment of the new Titan admiral and the maximum fleet strength he could have brought here. The spacecraft carrier *Vespa* is the flagship of the Titan Battle Fleet's new Commander-in-Chief, Admiral Vvorn. The *Vespa* is a powerful carrier of their latest design. They will have trained their pilots to perfection and upgraded their starfighters. Probably they will be in high spirits and very confident. We can estimate they brought together all their capital ships, including between four to six carriers that formed the tip of their spear. Behind them could be up to six monster dreadnaughts along with many escorts."

She added, "Here is a breakdown of the maximum strength Vvorn's fleet could have if they assembled nearly every warship from their empire for this all-or-nothing attack."

>
> Titan—Battle Fleet
> Admiral Vvorn
>   6 Spacecraft Carriers – 6 *Vespa* Class
>   Starfighter Space Wing
>   472 Fighters
>   472 Bombers
>   48 Recon
>   6 Dreadnought
>   6 Battlecruisers
>   136 Cruisers
>   188 Destroyers
>   188 Auxiliary Support Ships

"How much faith do you have in those estimates?" asked Gallant. "That would leave their own stars almost defenseless."

McCall shrugged, "We must plan for the worst-case scenario. Nothing else makes sense. Their intention will be to avenge the destruction of the Zzey battle fleet and bring our people down."

"What can you tell me of their fleet commander?"

"We've scanned the Titan communications and records and have constructed a fair estimate of Admiral Vvorn's curriculum vitae. He is a Titan with powerful shoulders and a slim waist. He likes to lean forward, poised on the balls of his feet as if ready to pounce. True to his heritage, he is a brilliant autistic savant. Logic and meticulous calculation are his forte. Despite keeping to doctrine, he has innovative talents that mark him unique amongst Titans. So, he hates any comparisons with his predecessor, Admiral Zzey. The Titan high command has unrestrained faith in him, and he will fight with total commitment. His staff officers are tactically excellent. He will have a master plan to succeed and distinguish him above all others."

A sensor operator interrupted, "We've some target data, sir."

It indicated that the Titan fleet was within striking distance of Earth.

"I'm betting that the *Cheshire's* sighting caused the Titans to launch prematurely," said McCall.

Gallant visualized the Titan admiral ordering, "Launch, launch, launch!"

The communication officer reported, "Sir, we

are picking up Earth news broadcasts from yesterday."

Gallant listened to the horrible news reports with corresponding waves of anguish.

It was just past noon when the *Cheshire's* message was broadcast over the *Constellation's* intercom for the crew. The Titans had attacked Earth's Home Fleet orbiting Earth's moon. The terrible media details were hard to listen to.

The deep rich baritone voice of the newscaster spoke with solemnity and compassion. "On Sunday, the Titan battle fleet of six carriers launched its starfighters to attack Earth's moon base. Several waves of enemy starfighters swept over that base and shot up our defensive combat units. They concentrated their assault on the main fleet base, Armstrong Luna."

The radio reports said, "It appears that their first wave was devastating. They branched out to hit as many critical targets as possible and disable essential defenses."

Fear blanketed Gallant's mind as the thought occurred to him that he might be about to witness the destruction of the Earth!

Alaina?

It was as if a man were sleeping peacefully at home only to awake suddenly to the sound of intruders breaking into his house. Before he could toss off the bedcovers, knives and clubs were stabbing and banging him into insensibility. He wouldn't have the slightest chance of getting out of bed and standing to his own defense. There would be no time to catch up. It would be too late. The assault would be overwhelmingly brutal and lethal.

He watched the bridge crew as they reacted and recoiled with each word of the news report. The stakes were high. He wondered what he could do to ease their pain.

The sense of personal loss struck him like a sledgehammer. He imagined a stain on his personal honor because he was aware that the Titans were prone to sneak attacks. Their acquisition of the Chameleon stealth technology had given them a chance they couldn't pass up. He guessed that the halo detection capability that he had forwarded to Earth months earlier was probably lying idle in a research lab. The fact that he was sitting in space too far from the action to be helpful left him utterly sickened. He suffered a sense of grief that he had never experienced before.

Gallant entered the CIC and pulled a neural interface cap over his head. Interacting with the ship's AI, he scanned the Earth sensor data, desperate to glean every possible clue from the data streaming his way. Over the course of the next several hours, he was able to piece together enough sensor data and radio communication to get a rough sense of the battle.

The Titans had sent reconnaissance to lead the first wave and report on fleet composition and location. Vvorn must have compiled a substantial intelligence report on the defenses. The first wave Titan assault was perfection. It targeted the critical defenses with the intent of incapacitating them.

As the wave of starfighters approached Earth's moon, they encountered and shot down most of the

CAP fighters. At least one of these radioed a somewhat incoherent warning. Other warnings confirmed the attacking starfighters had begun bombing and strafing. Nevertheless, it is not clear any warnings would have had much effect even if they had been interpreted correctly and much more promptly. The Titans achieved total dominance.

Fighters strafed and destroyed many of the fighters as they prepared to launch. The Moon's fighter bases never got into action. They never got up to intercept the Titan bombers. Blow after blow crippled the infrastructure of defensive weapons, communications, and computers. The battle was already decided after the first wave.

The United Planets always kept one dreadnaught and a cruiser destroyer division on alert to protect the Moon. It was this force that first confronted the Titan fleet, despite facing odds of twenty to one. It was swiftly annihilated.

The starfighter wave next attacked the capital ships with specially adapted missiles. The crews selected the highest value targets of the Home Fleet.

1st Fleet

Fleet Admiral Simone L. Graves

    4 Spacecraft Carriers – *Arc Royal, Eagle, Hermes, Lexington*

    4 Dreadnoughts – *Conqueror, Colossus, Defiant, Superb*

    4 Battlecruisers – *Achilles, Agamemnon, Arduous, Audacious*

>   24 Cruisers
>   48 Destroyers
>   2 Stealth Recon – *Cheshire*, *Siren*
>   72 Auxiliary Support Ships

Admiral Graves was unprepared for such an attack. At the very least, he could have expedited the use of the halo detection system. He should have deployed adequate sensor arrays to forewarn against a Titan sneak attack. He could have kept a portion of the fleet at full power rather than at standby. But instead, the whole fleet sat idling in orbit around the Moon bases with much of their crews on liberty, unable to respond to the battle station's alarm. The flagship, *Superb*, exploded during the first wave of the attack. Undoubtedly, Admiral Graves paid for his negligence with his life. The battle stations were likewise understaffed and ill-prepared. They were some of the first casualties of the Titan missiles.

The Titans found the Home Fleet in a complete failure of command and control. It illustrated what happened when leaders failed to do their jobs and instead left themselves vulnerable to danger. Men aboard UP ships awoke to the sounds of alarms, bombs exploding, and gunfire. The bleary-eyed men dressed as they ran to general quarters stations. Ammunition lockers were locked, starfighters were parked wingtip to wingtip in the hanger bays, and ships power plants were on standby.

Gallant pictured how the attack unfolded. He listened to the radio chatter, reviewed telemetry plots, and analyzed sensor data, all of which were already a day old. The radar and sensor images showed mere flashing-colored dots and arrow vectors. However, the audio radio chatter made the battle come alive.

One starfighter reported, "Captain, a large formation of ships approaching Earth bearing 092 mark2, range nine light-minutes."

Another starfighter reported, "Missiles launches are visible."

One starfighter said, "Damn, there are bogeys everywhere."

The desperation of the fighter chatter cast the grim struggle in human terms.

"I've lost my wingman. I'm blind, and I just got spiked."

They intermittently received faint static-filled signals.

"My radar is bent. Can anyone vector me clear?"

One after another, the starfighters pleaded for help.

"No angels near my position. Where is everyone? I have a bandit closing on my six."

As some signals faded, others popped up.

"I've been washed by a near miss. I'm bugging out and RTB."

And more.

"I've got this bird firewalled, and I can't get away from an enveloping ring of bandits. I'm a grape."

The fighter portion of the attack began at the starfighter pads, the largest, the main fighter base. The starfighters in the wave attacked the field on the sunward side. The only opposition came from a handful of CAP from the carriers.

The Home Fleet ships brought their engines to full power to depart orbit. It was too late. They came under direct assault of the Titan bombers. Missiles began to burst all around their frantic maneuvering.

Gallant followed the chatter that reached him a day after the events had taken place. He followed the CIC plot of the ships as the attack progressed. The tracks were chaotic and uncoordinated.

Once more, the radio transmissions told a bleak story. The ship chatter was equally grim.

The *Lexington* reported, "We're under heavy attack from starfighters. Nuclear missiles are hitting."

The *Hermes* reported, "Our escort cruiser blew up."

"We have a confusing radar picture. We can't tell friend from foe. We're playing blind man's bluff."

The Titans played their cards well and concentrated on the carriers first.

The *Colossus* reported, "The *Arc Royal* has been caught flatfooted by several missiles."

The *Defiant* asked, "What can we do to help?"

The *Arduous* called to the flagship, "I will be unable to power up for thirty minutes. What should I do?"

Rally around me. We're charging forward," radioed the *Conqueror* radioed.

The *Audacious* begged, "We've lost all power. We are adrift and launching escape pods. Send rescue."

They got no reply.

One cruiser destroyer squadron got underway. They reported, "All weapons stations manned and request targeting information."

The flagship replied, "Fire at any available target. We have an enemy dreadnaught dead ahead."

Nothing was easy. They knew they were in trouble. A missile exploded nearby and destroyed the ship. There was a nightmare of video images and shouts from his ship over the next few minutes. He began to maneuver away from the damaged ships and into the clear space beyond.

In an oddly disconnected voice, one officer reported, "I have a concussion. I'm hit. Got to keep firing."

"We're going to make it," shouted someone. Then a brilliant explosion marked his last location.

The Titan wave concentrated on the carriers but then shifted to the dreadnaughts. They launched numerous armor-piercing multiwarhead nuclear bombs to hit their intended dreadnaught targets. Several detonated before penetrating an armored deck. The Titan railguns were particularly effective in hitting the dreadnaughts.

As a mere spectator to the replaying of the event, Gallant could imagine how Vice-Admiral Simon L. Graves had responded to the attack. He pictured Graves as he received the news. Graves would have leaned against his overstuffed chair in his stateroom aboard his flagship, the *Superb*. His pitted red skin would have been dripping sweat into his bushy eyebrows and down his twitchy jowls. When he heard the bad news, he might have stuck his chin out to ask, "Are you certain? I refuse to believe you have accurately assessed the situation."

Already damaged by a missile and on-fire amidships, the *Arc Royal* attempted to exit the area. She was targeted by many Titan bombers as she got underway and sustained more hits from bombs, which started further fires. Several bulkheads were torn and ruptured from missiles knifing through her innards. She was hit by two more within minutes of each other. The smoke and fire were quickly out of control and rampaging throughout the upper deck. Starfighters were destroyed in her hanger without an opportunity to join the battle.

But it wasn't just a clash of titanium steel ships. There were real people inside those punctured burning hulks.

Seaman Peter Marshall of the *Arc Royal* joined a group in the mess hall which was serving as a medic station. He helped carry the wounded to tables where doctors treated them. He had only been aboard for a few weeks and was still learning his way through the many corridors. Nevertheless, he weaved his way from the hanger deck to the medic station, time and time again, carrying the wounded. At times he thought his arms would fall off, but he went back and forth without rest.

The *Colossus* was holed twice by missiles. Nevertheless, she plowed forward, determined to engage the enemy. She was surrounded by jammers and countermeasures she had emitted, but they did little good. She was moving too slow for them to be more effective.

Seaman Hale, a mechanic on the *Colossus* who had been on KP duty for not cleaning his station, ran to the nearest weapon station to help load ammunition. He found the area in chaos with railgun shells scattered all over the deck. Illogically, he fell to the deck, grabbing haphazardly at the shells with no idea how to load them.

"Stop that, you idiot, and help me with this magazine," said a nearby chief.

The *Conqueror* and *Defiant* were hit by four missiles, and the last two penetrated their armor. Great ribbons of streaming air hissed out into space. An oil tank streamed hydraulic fluid beside it.

But there was courage as well as confused fear and panic. A medic on the *Conqueror* ignored the sobs and screams of pain while he slapped a patch over a burn victim's leg. He worked feverishly to apply a tourniquet to the other leg. Syringes full of synthetic morphine derivatives were administered. There were all kinds of wounds and blood and dust from the area. They were trying to relieve the pain and suffering, but many were in shock. The conditions were terrible and unforgiving.

Fires erupted everywhere on the *Defiant*. Lieutenant Richards was so overtaken by the smoke he couldn't see or breathe. He reached out for the bulkhead to guide him along the corridor to the exit hatch.

He lurched through from compartment to compartment, but none was clear. Finally, a rescue worker grabbed him and pulled him to safety.

Lexington was hit by two of the nuclear cluster bombs; both caused serious damage.

Charles Browning, a communication specialist on the *Lexington,* was running to the CIC when an explosion knocked him off stride, and he fell down a hatch.

"Get off of me, you damn fool," shouted the partially dressed seaman that he landed on. They never got up. The next moment an explosion obliterated the compartment.

Hermes was hit by seven missiles, the seventh tearing away her thrusters.

Marine Sargent Carlos Perez of the *Hermes* jumped out of the way of flying shards of metal. He sought to find shelter in the next compartment only to find it had been ruptured, and the atmosphere was fast disappearing. Holding his breath, he turned and clawed his way back. He tried to seal the compartment, but he couldn't hold his breath long enough and succumbed to suffocation.

Eagle was hit by two bombs and two missiles. The ship shuddered and staggered forward like a drunk leaving a bar.

When nurse Conners of the *Eagle* fell to the deck after a blow to the head, she thought she would die right there. But she was able to stagger to her feet and made her way to the medic stand where patients were piled up. A doctor said, don't take anymore. We are full. She ministered to as many as she could over the next few minutes, but all her efforts came to naught when a missile hit the compartment.

One injured woman was quietly sobbing.

Conners said, "Don't worry, Mary. It will be all right. Everything is going to be all right."

The crew might have kept the *Eagle* fighting, but the damage grew beyond their control. Soon they were ordered to abandon ship. Burning oil covered her inner decks and made the situation worse.

A great many of the crew were young men and women, untried in life and untested in combat. Lorretta Setter was a bomber pilot from the *Eagle* who was scheduled to test fly her ship. When the battle began, she climbed aboard her Viper II.

Her Chief said, "You have only one heavy missile and half your countermeasures loaded."

She said, "Doesn't matter, Chief. Rev her up. I'm going."

She flew straight into the thick of the action. She was swamped by enemy fighters but strangely they all passed her by looking for juicier targets. She was the lone bomber to reach the enemy fleet and fire her one Goliath missile, which hit an enemy dreadnaught.

Although the Titans concentrated on the capital ships, they did not ignore other targets. The cruisers were hit by missiles. Many destroyers were destroyed when bombs reached their orbit.

Of the United Planets 402 starfighters, 136 were destroyed and 155 damaged and rendered useless. Almost none took off to defend the base. Only fifty-five Titan starfighters were shot down during the attack.

Just as the Home Fleet ships gathered speed and tried to get into formation, they had to dodge the starfighters of another wave. This was followed by the Titan battle line dreadnaughts, which launched a massive missile strike that proved to be the final blow to eliminate the fleet.

In a matter of a few short, violent hours, the Home Fleet was crushed. Mere minutes after the last explosions of the devastating battle, the world was changed forever. The people of Earth were staring ruin in the face. They could be the next target.

Would they be bombarded?
Would they be invaded?
Were they doomed?

CHAPTER 4

Fools Rush In

Framed within the open hatch, Henry Gallant observed the bridge of the UPSS *Constellation* CVS-647. Despite her battle scars and imperfections, she remained his pride and joy. It was 08:04. Four minutes past the change of the morning watch, and the commotion on the bridge had died down to a hushed calm. Consciously, he inhaled, filling his lungs with the peculiar oily scent of recycled air. Tall, sparse, and as tough as the titanium alloy that forged his ship, he set his jaw.

The destruction of the Home Fleet was a bitter pill for Gallant to swallow, but it wasn't the only one.

He had to ask himself why Earth had received insufficient warning? And why he was so far away when the disaster occurred? Could the possibility of the destruction of the fleet been foreseen?

Gallant had hoped that peace was possible and that all would be safe given the halo detectors he had sent to Earth. But he might have anticipated that Admiral Graves would be slow to implement the devices. He knew enough about the aliens to understand their devious nature. He might have expected that peace was going to be difficult to achieve. He should have foreseen the Titan's violent behavior. So, he knew where at least some of the fault lay. He shrunk from dwelling on the thought that this was, at least in part, the consequences of his miscalculations. Calculations he should have gotten right but hadn't.

There it was.

The second bitter pill laid bare—his personal failure.

Now he had to pull himself together. Recrimination would be plentiful in days to come. There was no point reliving an opportunity missed. It was necessary to find a way forward to minimize the damage and make amends. There was still a chance to redeem himself if he made the right moves going forward.

Through the static interference from the solar flare, he could make out radar blips. These were targets of concern, but this was an uncertain moment on the bridge. Everything was in suspended animation.

Gallant's duty was before him. He must act to protect and defend the people of Earth. He felt ready to meet that challenge. But as he approached his command chair, Captain Julie Ann McCall stepped in front of him.

"No!" Shaking her head emphatically, McCall said, "I know what you're thinking. But even if Task Force 34 were in peak condition, it's no match for

Vvorn's fleet. You can't do it. We can't do it. I wish we could, but we can't. Every rational thought screams we shouldn't."

"Ha, h'm," he mumbled.

When he had first arrived in the Solar System, Gallant had assumed the posture of a peacetime military officer. He had looked forward to enjoying his wife's company. Now he was unprepared for the jarring situation.

He had two damaged and depleted carriers with less than half of their normal compliment. Two battlecruisers in terrible condition with a cruiser destroyer escort that was as weak as a litter of kittens. His carriers alone were at thirty percent fighter capacity, and there would be a lot of new pilot training to undertake. Fortunately, he had outfitted the task force with the halo detectors that Kate Mahoney and Ensign Logan had developed. So, at least he wasn't flying blind.

Despite all that, he intended to accelerate toward the Titans.

He had to be resourceful in dealing with this problem. He had to engage and drive away a more powerful enemy before they could complete the destruction of Earth.

Gallant said, "Vvorn will detect us soon. He doesn't know our strength. He could assume that it might be from two to six carriers with two to six dreadnaughts, given their total capabilities. Vvorn, on the other hand, has just fought a major battle. True, he won, but he no longer has surprise on his side. He might have considerable ship damage and loss."

He paused and searched McCall's face for reassurance. There was none.

He continued, "Their weapons are low, and their crews are exhausted. He will see Task Force 34 accelerating straight for him, welcoming battle. The Earth battle stations and starfighters are still operational. They are formidable. He is not prepared to take them on as well as us. He has no occupation force to land on the moon. His was always a hit-and-run operation. Vvorn should be happy with his victory and disappear with his stealth technology. He can vanish into the asteroid belt and let us look for him. Hide and seek is his future. And that doesn't even count our forces returning from our stars, which should be undertaking a role in the coming days."

McCall's grimace was softening.

Gallant concluded, "Having crippled our forces, he can afford to look for a new strategic opportunity."

McCall remained doubtful but acknowledged, "The Titans are highly organized and ritualistic. When they're presented with a surprising dilemma, they often withdraw to reconsider their options. If we can look sufficiently menacing, they may hesitate and withdraw as you suggest."

Gallant said, "You don't think this task force should confront the enemy?"

McCall said, "Given the state these ships are in, I don't think this task force could confront a solar flare." She shook her head and added, "There is no hope."

Gallant didn't want to go back into battle. He didn't feel a damn bit courageous. In fact, at this moment, given the suddenness of the horrific news he had absorbed, he felt physically, emotionally, and psychologically vulnerable. But he had to pretend none of that was real. He stood in front of his bridge crew and had to appear as brave and as determined as they needed him to be.

He said, "There is always hope!"

I know what I must do!

Turning to the helmsman, Gallant ordered, "All ships, ahead full!"

As Task Force 34 sped full speed toward Earth, Gallant addressed his crew over the intercom. "We are going to face this enemy and save our homes."

Over the next few hours, he tracked the enemy fleet as it positioned itself near the moon as if to prepare for additional strikes. He was uncertain whether they would shift their attention to Earth.

Each passing hour brought the *Constellation* closer to Earth and to the Titan fleet.

Gallant had to wait and see whether his gambit would cause Vvorn to back away or come roaring at the tattered Task Force 34. It was a nerve-wracking, high-stakes gamble.

The Titans seemed to remain on hold.

The communication officer said, "Captain, we are receiving a current transmission from the *Cheshire*."

Gallant put it on audio.

"Task Force 34, this is picket ship, *Cheshire*. The

Home Fleet has been attacked by a Titan fleet. I picked up your distant signal and only now received your IFF signal to identify you. Command forgot about us, and we are looking to join any active units."

"Good, you're just in time. Join up"

Gallant asked CIC to calculate whether the Titans had detected his task force. "Most likely, they detected us an hours ago, Captain. But they would only be able to distinguish us as a large fleet formation. They wouldn't be able to distinguish individual ships or starfighters."

McCall said, "They would assume we were a fleet returning from another star system. They would be furious at their bad luck to be interrupted before they could finish their mission. Luck is everything, and it is funny how it always seeks balance."

Gallant said, "They would be debating if they should face us."

"Or they might consider gathering their damaged ships and changing course for the asteroids. That would let things stew and fret."

"They would never know what might come next, and with each passing day, we will grow stronger, and they will become weaker until the end."

"They have a reputation for planning. They must have planned for the attack on the solar system, including contingencies for moving into the outer planets."

Gallant said, "They probably had several major aims. First, they intended to destroy important fleet units. That would prevent the fleet from interfering with the Titan's conquest of the outer planets. Next, they wanted to deliver a blow to our ability to mobilize our capital ships. They hoped that the attack would undermine our morale, forcing the government to yield to the Titan's territorial demands. Vvorn must be concerned his force was now within range of Earth bombers. He is uncertain whether the United Planets had enough surviving starfighters to launch an attack against his carriers. He would not wish to risk further losses."

Gallant waited as Task Force 34 closed on the enemy fleet.

CHAPTER 5

Last Rites

When the *Constellation* reached the Moon, Gallant found that his assessment of the Home Fleet's battle was very close to what had transpired. With drooping eyes and a heavy heart, he surveyed the combat wreckage. He saw fragments of great ships. Space was littered with escape pods and bloated corpses. Some of the officers and crew he knew.

It was like walking in on a funeral. You're pleased to see those you care about are well, but the grief for those you've lost floods over you.

The Titans had succeeded in turning the Home Fleet into a Hellstrom and then departed. Gallant watched as their fading radar glow receded into the distance.

A news feed showed images of the battle from the ship's bridge video feed. A few seconds of bewilderment preceded a moment of horrid doubt before

Gallant understood what was on the viewscreen.

There are a hundred ways to get killed in battle, and Gallant had seen them all. The possibilities always held secrets of pain and horror. There are explosions, fires, suffocation, crashes, bullets, lasers, plasma, and collisions. Those are the obvious ones, but there are many others, less likely but just as final. He had nearly come to an uncomfortable end himself on more than one occasion.

Gaunt, dirty, and bloody survivors walked among the dead, trying to wash away the pain from their minds as well as their bodies. They were fixated on their loved ones and homes at this moment. The caskets of the dead were lined up in the overflowing morgues. Many were unidentified even by DNA matching. They had to reconcile with that as well.

How could Earth win when every loss builds the conviction that they are doomed to failure? They must have a belief that they will learn and adapt, grow and be better so that they could win.

Now that the crisis had come, it was an acute predicament for Gallant. His feelings toward the Titans were cold fury. He not only wanted them defeated, but he also wanted to be the one who did it. He wanted to smash them as completely as they had the Home Fleet. He gathered his wits to formulate a plan of action. He knew since the victory of Ross there was more work to be done, and he would have to be involved, but his timing was off. He hadn't reckoned with how swiftly the Titans could move.

Gallant wondered what to do next. Hope was

a sentiment he kept close. But he feared that after so much death, many might lose hope. He had a sudden secret premonition of dread that something had happened to Alaina. He wanted to rush to her.

He watched the news broadcast as it showed the individual ships of the fleet with ruptured hulls, bent frames, burnt-out compartments and hospital ships transporting the wounded planet-side for advanced care. Some of the ships were unhabitable, let alone functional. A few, being towed by their sister ships, were undergoing transfer to planet tugs. He could see the crew members straining at the bit to get ashore. He was sensitive to the appearance of the damage and suffering, but he couldn't minimize it. It was a badge of their courage in facing and fighting a powerful, determined enemy.

There was so much to do that Gallant knew he would not be able to leave the ship for hours, and Alaina would be waiting and waiting. He bit his tongue. He wanted to dump all the immediate work on Fletcher or someone else to free himself, but that wasn't his way. There were just some things that a leader had to deal with.

He prepared a report for the admiralty. He had messaged all the priority items. But he had to ensure that adequate sentry ships were guarding the area. And he had to ensure that the possibility of damaged ships exploding was eliminated. All this before he could consider leaving the ship.

So finally, when all was reasonably secure, he announced to the OOD that he was leaving. He took the shuttle to Earth and his home.

The news of the disaster was broadcast from all media outlets across the globe. One broadcaster said, "President Gerome Neumann has proclaimed that this day to be avenged. The Titans had sued for peace, and negotiations were underway in Melbourne. So, the betrayal is raw. The president said that help is on the way and that everything is on track to stabilize security."

The commentator looked at the camera and paused before adding, "The president has instructed fleet command to mobilize every asset for Earth's protection. They are developing contingency plans for every eventuality. He warned of the risks to shipping and outer planets. He urged all political parties to unite behind his efforts in this time of dire emergency."

The candor that this moment required would be difficult for any occupant of the presidency, but there were three things that Neumann and his government needed to acknowledge: first, actions were necessary to ensure Earth's security; second, reassurance of support must be given to the outer planets; and third, preparations were necessary to take the war to the enemy. Even if Neumann found the courage to acknowledge these hard truths, words wouldn't be enough. The administration also needed to announce specific actions to be taken.

The news cameras sprang to life to capture the

moment. A video feed showed the president standing statuesque in his suit. With Neumann's thoughts dancing over his face, the public saw him with his entourage standing before the podium. He spoke in hushed whispers and gestured for everyone to be quiet. But they weren't ready to settle down yet.

Neumann had received a briefing from the director of the SIA. He was told that the surprise attack, crippled the fleet. Titan fighters and bombers came in waves that were launched from six spacecraft carriers. There were enough to destroy or damage all the Home Fleet's six carriers and dreadnaughts. They also damaged or destroyed scores of cruisers and destroyers, as well as numerous space stations and satellites. A total of 388 starfighters were destroyed; all UP carriers and dreadnaughts were crippled or destroyed, 42,488 men and women were killed, and 81,178 others were wounded. Important base installations such as the power station, dry dock, shipyard, maintenance, and fuel facilities were destroyed. The Titan losses were light, leaving them free to launch attacks that stretched across Jupiter, Saturn, and the other star systems.

SIA estimated that although the Titans knew that the United Planets had ample resources to stage a comeback, they expected that with the Home Fleet crippled the Titans could reestablish themselves in the Solar System and eventually dominate it. They expected that they could strangle the planets through disrupting interplanetary commerce and break their will to resist. It never occurred to the Titans that there was anything morally wrong with their plans. They believed that their genetically superior species was inherently right to conquer. Hoping for a quick conquest, they formulated their plans accordingly. Now they would plot a course through the system to the outer planets with precision to avoid any bases that might reveal their path.

Now, Neumann had to face the people and give them a far different story to calm their fears.

He said, "It is with a heavy heart that I report the grave losses of the Home Fleet. Their courage is a tribute to our people in their ability to keep us safe with their last breath. We will investigate how this surprise attack was carried out, and we will punish the Titans."

The president paused and drew a deep breath before concluding, "For now, we are safe."

CHAPTER 6

Scapegoat

"Please come to see me at the soonest possible moment."

Gallant reread the message. It seemed less dire the second time.

Gallant had wanted to see the retired Admiral Collingsworth ever since he set foot on Earth, but he had been at a loss on how to arrange it without interference from fleet command. Now Admiral Collingsworth was waiting for him at his country estate. The situation was out of his hands. Any repercussions would be directed at the admiral rather than at him for any breach of protocol. He could envision that that was Collingsworth's intent. He still had to cope with an order to meet with fleet command later.

It's going to be an interesting day.

A few hours later, a marine led Gallant into Collingsworth's library.

"That will be all, Sergeant," said Collingsworth

dismissing the marine.

Gallant glanced around the room and was impressed with the collection of military memorabilia adorning the room. He could imagine the many battles and experiences of Collingsworth's lifetime achievements.

"Please be seated, Captain. Can I offer you a glass of wine?" asked the admiral seated in a comfortable chair beside an open window. Sunlight streamed into the room, offering an optimistic atmosphere.

"Ah, yes, thank you, sir."

The older man poured a glass of wine from a carafe.

Gallant took the glass and raised it. "To your good health, Admiral."

Collingsworth picked up his glass and responded, "And to yours."

Gallant took a long draw from the glass, nearly draining it before he realized how much he wanted it.

The admiral barely touched the liquid.

"My apologies for insisting on seeing you when I know how overwhelmed you are. I particularly wanted to speak to you before you were debriefed by fleet command, or you made your formal report to the political powers."

Gallant squirmed in his chair. This was getting awkward.

"I will be on my way to fleet headquarters the moment we are through here, sir. President Neumann has ordered me to gather the fleet remnants of the Home Fleet to join Task Force 34. Rear Admiral Butler has the only other substantial military force at Saturn. Because Admiral Graves is dead, he is consulting with the admiralty on a new command structure for the solar system."

"I understand. I shan't keep you long, but it's imperative that you hear what I have to convey."

"Of course, sir," said Gallant. "I have a preliminary draft of my action report for your review."

He placed the secret document on the nearby table.

"Thank you for that. I will read it after you've gone. For now, just give me the highlights."

"President Neumann is furious with the ability of the Titan fleet to sneak up upon us. I have detailed how the halo detectors were provided to Fleet Command. They made the decision to send the devices to a research lab rather than deploy them. Also, a picket ship, the *Cheshire,* did raise an alarm that was not fully appreciated by fleet command."

Collingsworth nodded. "Admiral Graves was a brave sailor, but he had his blind spots. I regret his loss."

"Yes, sir." Gallant appreciated how Collingsworth understood the situation without casting harsh aspersions.

Collingsworth said, "President Neumann is as much a force of nature as a powerful leader. He exerts his control like a force of gravity. While his machinations distract the eye like shiny baubles, his actual intentions are often unobserved. Because the war has continued to slide downhill, we can expect him to issue an address to the people to reassure them and restore faith in his government. Perhaps most broadly, the flawed response to the Titan attack has diminished his authority. He must show that his judgment going forward will be sound."

"I understand," said Gallant.

After nearly a decade of war, the people had adapted amazingly well to the changing circumstance. However, there was always the problem of one disaster too many for any population, and reality had dealt them a bitter hand. The future held several disturbing possibilities. But over time an improving security picture for the thirty billion inhabitants of Earth would mean there would be flexibility on how to proceed. Earth now faced the compounding challenge of emergency calls and the threat of economic collapse.

"President Neumann met with his cabinet and military leaders to demonstrate their resolve. The government has sent recall ships out to the other star systems with task forces, which were ordered to return to the solar system," said Gallant.

Collingsworth said, "However, in war, as in many human endeavors, the law of unintended consequences is often cruel and unrelenting. So, as you contend with the fallout of the disastrous loss of the Home Fleet, you will also face rising political angst searching for a scapegoat. As a Natural, you fit the bill."

"Why do you think I will face disapproval?"

The admiral said, "Didn't you report that the

Chameleon and the Titan were finished off in the Ross star system? They may say that this is your fault."

Gallant said, "But the treaty failure and the failure to use the Halo detectors are exculpatory."

"The admiralty will conclude that they can't replace you immediately without cause. It would appear very drastic. They will wait. Things are bad and likely to get worse. They will wait until you make a misstep, and then act."

Gallant said, "The president also insinuated that I might have been quicker to arrive and done more to pursue the enemy."

"Ha. You had the good fortune to turn up at just the right moment to save Earth," said Collingsworth.

"But not in time to save the Home Fleet."

"Somethings are beyond the fates of chance, even for the noblest of men. You could have turned a blind eye and stayed clear of the battle considering the condition and composition of your limited force. But after your exploits of the past year, the Titans may have learned to be wary of Task Force 34."

Gallant leaned back in his chair.

"Your arrival was really a magnificent sight. It was broadcast over the media, and the public was ecstatic. You did well to drive them away."

"Thank you, sir, I suspect our sudden appearance was a significant shock. They are no doubt reassessing how powerful my task force is."

"Yes, ... yes that is true. While their battle fleet withdrew when you confronted it, they will return to threaten Earth and Mars. You must be prepared for them when they do."

Gallant furrowed his brow. "Yes, sir. I will be."

"I suspect that the Titan attack on the Home Fleet was only the opening salvo of a much larger campaign."

"Then you don't see this as a hit-and-run operation?"

"No, not at all. I believe that we will soon learn that the outer planets will also be attacked as part of the Titan's plan to reoccupy them."

"That makes perfect sense."

"Good, good," said Collingsworth before he took a great gulp of his wine. "I believe that I should be recalled to duty as soon as possible so that I may help repel this invasion."

Gallant said, "That would be wonderful, sir. You should return as commander-in-chief of the fleet, sir."

"No, no. The fleet is in your capable hands. You will need me here on Earth overseeing the planet's defenses and marshaling all available resources to assist you."

Gallant almost blushed.

"How may I be of service?"

"I'm certain you appreciate there will be military and political opposition to my returning to active duty."

"I could imagine that to be true, but surely under the circumstance, no one would dream of keeping our finest leader on the sideline. Not while we face an existential threat."

"You might think so, but I am afraid that is what will happen without your explicit intervention."

Gallant grimaced.

"What is the condition of your task force?"

"We are replenishing and hope to return to full strength, though we still do not have a full complement of starfighters. The ships are in bad need of a refit as well. But fully functional."

"How many ships of the Home Fleet have joined you?"

"Several scores of cruisers and destroyers."

"Carriers? Dreadnaughts?"

"None."

"Were they all destroyed?" asked the shocked and dismayed admiral.

"Most were, but there are many cripples that may yet be salvaged though it will take considerable time. We might have a carrier and a dreadnaught operational in four to six months. I've sent messages to our task forces in other star systems to send us reinforcements. But until they arrive there is only what I've gathered here and the squadrons guarding the outer planets." He tried not to betray his anxiety as he added, "If we can hold out until then."

"What is the strength of those squadrons?"

"Jupiter has one dreadnaught and a supporting battlecruiser and destroyer escort. Saturn has only two battlecruisers and a cruiser destroyer escort under Admiral Butler. The starfighter strength is likewise minimal."

"You should leave them in place, if possible,

until the last moment."

"Will do, sir."

"And the Titan fleet?

"It vanished. Their stealth is good enough to hide their fleet even from halo detectors if they keep a fair distance. My guess is that they withdrew to the asteroids where they will reestablish their old bases. From there they can wreak havoc on our shipping and outer planets. The methane moons of Saturn would be an appealing target for them to reoccupy," said Gallant.

Collingsworth said, "I think that's a reasonable assessment, and certainly a good starting point until we acquire more information. However, I would suggest one more wrinkle. I would bet that Vvorn had orders to release one or two of his carriers to return to Gliese soon after he delivered his blow against the Home Fleet. If I were in the Titan high command, I wouldn't gamble by leaving my home world naked any longer than was absolutely necessary."

Gallant nodded, "I agree, sir. They gambled to get a major strategic advantage. Now is the time to count their chips and plan for the next encounter. If they have already detached two carriers to Gliese, then there are still four carriers roaming around the outer planets. I am preparing to dispatch my four stealth reconnaissance ships, the *Warrior, Invidia, Siren,* and *Cheshire,* to pursue them through the asteroids and beyond. Hopefully, they can give us a better picture of the enemy's disposition before too long."

"That's good, Henry. Good," said Collingsworth. He licked his lips and added, "Now I need to raise a rather delicate matter with you. I need your help to get reinstated to active duty. That will only happen if you make a firm demand to both the admiralty and the president."

Gallant set his jaw as he said, "I will, sir."

There was a twinkle in Collingsworth's crystal blue eyes. "Don't be so eager to put your head in the noose, Henry. Advocating my return to duty will meet great resistance, and you may be threatened. They may consider removing you, though I personally put that in the category of an unrealized threat. You are too well-known now. Your victory at Ross and your fortuitously timed return made you politically difficult to fire. They may threaten it, but it is unlikely they will be brave enough to carry it out. To that end, you must be persistent enough to wait them out."

Gallant could see the need and believed it was worthwhile. He needed Collingsworth backing him up at home while he chased the Titan battle fleet.

"Do your best."

"I will, sir."

"We'll meet again. Remember, do nothing that leaves Earth defenseless. Your first duty is to safeguard our people."

"I understand, sir."

"And take a moment to convey my best to your wife." he exclaimed. "You've been deployed a long time. You must be anxious to spend whatever planetside time you have with your her."

"Yes, sir. I was going to squeeze a few hours

with her before returning to the *Constellation*."

"I'm sorry for delaying you this long."

"It was necessary, admiral."

"Your good wife will not be pleased if I keep you longer."

"I'll make amends, sir."

"It's I who must beg her pardon, and if you permit, my wife and I will see that she is well provided for while you are absent."

"That is most kind of you, sir. I'm sure she would appreciate your support. Though you and your wife may find she is a curious soul and likely to have more requests than you can anticipate."

"Ha, ha. I will look forward to that. In any case, once I am reinstated, I expect to get a long list of needs from you. I promise to act quickly to see them fulfilled."

"Thank you, Admiral."

CHAPTER 7

Magical

After spending months looking forward to returning home, after all the build-up, it's impossible not to have high hopes for a special moment. And that first hello, that first kiss, really should be amazing.

A warm image of Alaina flickered into Gallant's mind, but it was disrupted by the memory of their last bitter quarrel on the day he left for deployment. But as he entered his home, Alaina was quick to greet him.

Their eyes met. A tiny smile cracked from the edge of her mouth as she said, "Hello, Stranger."

Gallant almost laughed but restrained his response to, "I hope we're not going to remain strangers."

Standing before Alaina for the first time in over a year, Gallant was uncertain. It was awkward. For starters, people changed after long absences. And there had been much left unsaid on their parting.

That's a reality that has taken every military spouse by surprise at one point or another. But an extended period apart, especially one so emotionally significant, will change both partners. Returning spouses often feel out of sync with their families. Some plan a celebration, but feelings of joy, excitement, and anxiety overflow into a collage of mixed emotions.

Gallant was certain that Alaina had quietly made herself crazy over whether he would come home in one piece or not. She had been working as a journalist for the last year, and that involved its own hardships. Annoyingly her life had gone on without him. He wondered how she would deal with their new situation.

He had always been inspired to service by a sense of something bigger than himself. Something more important. Call it a yearning based upon self-sacrifice. He considered it illogical to some degree, but it was always there. Now he had to face it all again, and he had to know she was in this with him.

Alaina reached up and brushed back a lock of hair from his forehead. The unbridled happiness on her face nearly stopped his heart. Her broad smile and huge bright eyes showed she was expecting a kiss.

Gallant leaned closer. Their lips gently touched and lingered. He wrapped his arms around her and pulled her close. They stayed entwined, breathing rhythmically for a long pleasing moment.

It was as magical as their first time. They were lovers once more.

He was happy. It seemed his worries about

their relationship were misplaced. He was conscious of her trembling body as she smothered him with more kisses. She was melting with happiness. He returned her passion with a bear hug as he twirled her around.

It's wonderful to be home.

"Oh, Henry."

He hadn't heard his first name spoken in over a year, and he liked the way she said it. A warm intimacy washed over him. He was at home, at peace. For several seconds, he smiled at her, and she at him. He agonized over telling her that his visit would be short, less than twelve hours. He couldn't utter the words that would shatter her joy.

But after reunion comes renewal—and while both are exciting, renewal is harder than it might seem. Adjustments take time. He didn't have that.

If he had a grain of sense, he would resign and stay home forever. But that was not an option. He stood like a statue until she said, "I know you don't have much time, but I've made dinner, and I was hoping you could stay the night.

He merely nodded. She understood.

His next thoughts were of Alaina and their relationship. He had been gone for nearly a year again. She hated that. He would have to devote serious time to rebuild their relationship and keep their communication strong. She accepted the difficulties of being a military spouse. He needed to give her what was necessary for her to be happy.

She marched him into the dining room and

began bringing dishes from the kitchen. She kept up a continuous stream of chatter throughout the meal. Most of it was of little consequence, but all of it was comfortably transporting them back to their life as a couple with familiar ideas and feelings. By the time they went to bed, it was as an old married couple returning to the passion they hadn't forgotten.

Sometimes he felt he lacked the hot spicy ingredients she craved. He needed to capture her happiness. He was bold in battle, but perhaps he lacked something in love. Alaina could say, but she didn't.

Does she love me back?

Gallant suffered from the fear that she openly adored him, but that she was secretly hurt when he didn't quite measure up to her needs. Such as his lack of concern about his absences. Or his reluctance to embrace fatherhood.

In the morning, Alaina said she had something important to discuss with him. Her solemn composure worried him, for the topic could be any of several disturbing subjects. One in particular worried him.

"There has been social unrest on Earth since you left. It's been about the genetic engineering laws. I've been a reporter assigned to cover it, and it's been difficult."

"Do I need to worry?"

"There are people who do not see you as a hero but rather as an enemy. I'm talking about those who take genetic engineering overly seriously."

She said, "Sometimes, I hate the work I do. I want to do something important, particularly now. I want my effort to matter. Reporting on the social troubles of our people is valuable, but is it essential?"

"Is there something else of concern you're not telling me?"

"Yes. But not now. I will discuss it with you as soon as I can."

He wanted to stay and comfort her, but he could not stay away from his command any longer.

He said, "I must go. Can this wait so we can discuss this another time?"

She nodded and added, "Here, sit and eat your breakfast." She coaxed him into a chair.

"I'm not really hungry, but I'd love a cup of coffee. I'll sit with you for a few minutes."

He took the cup as she poured the steaming hot liquid.

He took a great gulp that scorched his mouth, but he said nothing and took another swig.

"Don't worry. I won't take unnecessary risks, and I will return soon."

She said, "Everyone has pain in their past. I find that being open about it makes it easier to bear. You can share your burden with me."

He said, "When I first had a command, I worried that I wasn't up to the task. Then I accepted the responsibility. I know that when we are facing a situation, we must focus on the ones we are saving, even if there are others that are sacrificed. It's an ugly thought, but there is no turning it aside. You learn to live with it."

"Are you always so unflinchingly brave?" Alaina reached up and brushed a lock of hair off his forehead.

"No. Actually, I've had my dark and trembling moments. Fortunately, they pass. So far, I haven't let myself down. But I know there are more of those moments waiting for me. I'll have to face them again. Out there. Somewhere."

"Darling, I know you must go, but you must . . ."

"I'll return as soon. Nothing shall keep me from you, my dear."

Alaina, pleaded, "Henry, we need to talk. Maybe not now, but soon. You know why. We must talk about it. It's important to both of us."

What? What did she need? Could he fulfill her desires? He wanted to say the right words to comfort her and show his tender feelings.

He tried to strike the correct tone. "We will. I promise. Please be patient."

CHAPTER 8

Recon

The next day, Gallant met with the captains of the *Warrior*, the *Invidia*, the *Cheshire*, and the *Siren*, in the wardroom of the *Constellation*. They were a collection of talented officers with serious but eager faces. Gallant had confidence in his old friend, John Roberts, and intended to give him the most critical job. He was also impressed with how Charles Jaeger of the *Cheshire h*ad handled himself during his encounter with the Titan fleet. Jaeger would be assigned the next toughest task. The other men were unknown to Gallant, but he hoped they would be up to the challenge he was going to give them.

"Gentlemen, the Titans have disappeared into the cosmos." He waited a beat to let that sink in. "Your job will be to find them and learn what they are up to. Your reconnaissance ships have the finest stealth capabilities in existence. Your halo sensors are the best detectors possible. Together those capabilities will allow you to penetrate undetected into the Titans hiding places and gather intelligence on their disposition and operations."

Again, he paused. He watched their individual faces contort as they calculated what they might face.

"In effect, you will become the eyes and ears of our space navy."

Though the room was at a comfortable temperature and coffee had been served, the gathering remained uneasy. Citations and awards of the ship's battles hung on the wall. They were reminders of the battles that the *Constellation* had fought and the losses she had suffered. The names of fallen crew members were inscribed on the tabletop. A painting depicting the ship in battle ran the length and width of the back wall. Everything was a reminder that the participants' encounters would face daunting comparisons.

Gallant continued, "You will be operating individually far from support and relying on your own discretion. I expect you to keep tabs on the number and types of units in your assigned area and monitor their communications. You will send me regular updates as well as your own assessment of the local situation. I expect you to dig deep and offer real insights into the Titans objectives."

A look of consternation passed around the room.

"Some of you may be uncomfortable about revealing your personal prognosis with meager information. But that is what I need. You will be on the front lines. You will have the best view even if it is sparse. I don't expect you to be right all the time, but I will rely on what you think to form my own conclusion. So do your best."

"There were still some looks of concern. Gallant noticed that Jaeger showed a hint of smile at the corners of his mouth. He liked that.

Roberts shifted uncomfortably in his seat. "Sir, we've been unable to decrypt the Titans code since they adopted their new cyphers."

"True," said Gallant, casting his eyes on Roberts. "That's because the Titans have upgraded their networks to use a hybrid Titan Chameleon AI encryption. It's completely stymied the SIA. It has us beat for the moment. For now, we can only collect their transmission without being able to decipher them. But I have plans to change that eventually."

Roberts seemed relieved.

"I am especially interested in finding their communication relay boxes for the express purpose of breaking that code," said Gallant.

There were several nodding heads.

Gallant said, "I have mapped out a search plan to find and track the Titan fleet. It breaks into several elements each accomplishing different tasks. I am assigning Captain John Roberts of the *Warrior* and Captain Burt Valdez of the *Invidia* to sweep the asteroid fields. The Titans will likely use the asteroids to establish bases for raiding our commerce, facilitating their communication network, and storing replenishment food and weapon supplies."

"John, I am giving you an additional assignment of establishing a code breaking station expressly to decrypt the Titan communications."

"Ahh?" Roberts sounded hesitant. But then, he quickly added, "Will do, sir."

"You will take decryption experts Kate Mahoney and Ensign Daniel Logan with you along with their quantum computer equipment."

Roberts visibly relaxed. "Yes, sir."

"The XO and I have combed through the CIC data to check for potential locations. The asteroid belt included many asymmetrical rocky bodies that might serve. Three smaller clusters skirt the outer edges with some asteroids more than several kilometers wide."

He pointed to a cluster near the outer perimeter of the field. "You should start here."

"Aye aye, sir."

The captains leaned forward, eager to learn more about their assignment.

Gallant added, "Captain Charles Jaeger of The *Cheshire*, and Captain Val Chin of the *Siren* will range toward Saturn and Jupiter respectively. You are to investigate the reoccupation of old Titan facilities and keep an eye on our bases in the area. You'll have to set up charging stations and listening posts throughout the region."

Chin asked, "Why can't we use our existing stations, sir?"

"The Titans have had spy drones in the system for years. They probably have as good a map of our bases as we have."

The captains nodded their understanding.

"Well, gentlemen, that's your assignment. I've placed a heavy burden upon your shoulders, but I am confident you will succeed."

Over the course of the next week, they pursued their assignments. Most led to false trails.

Two weeks later, Captain John Roberts spent every waking minute on the bridge as his ship conducted an extensive search. The asteroid fields varied in density. Mostly there was just empty space with a few rocks scattered around, but in some areas, clusters of asteroids blocked radar signals. But space is big, and when you're looking for a needle in a haystack the odds are against you. Yet, he was not looking for a dumb needle randomly left in a haystack. He was looking for a very smart enemy with a specific agenda. There were areas of high probability where the Titans would go either for opportunity or mischief. Therefore, Robert tailored his hunt to counter the most dangerous efforts.

He considered how the war had changed over the years and how that might affect his decision about where he should concentrate. Years earlier in 2151, when the war first started, the Titans attempted to claim the outer planets of the Solar System. They had established great cities and bases throughout the Saturn moons and beyond. But when they tried to attack Jupiter, they were repulsed by Admiral Collingsworth's fleet. Then for several years the war festered while interstellar travel drives were developed. At that point, the war took on new dimensions with several star systems invaded and attacked. The Titans were forced to evacuate their colonies in the solar system.

Focus shifted to the strategically important Ross system. The complications of the Chameleon civilization had been an additional problem over the last few years. It was Gallant who saved the marines at Ross and led a mission against the Gliese star system. That was followed by his decisive defeat of the Chameleon and the main Titan battle fleet at Ross, which seemed to end things. The Titans said they wanted peace, but they lied. Now they were coming back to their old haunts.

Maintaining stealth mode, the *Warrior* approached the outer edge of the asteroid belt. She was surrounded by a rock cluster family, thousands of asteroids in all sizes and shapes. The high density of asteroids created a nest of rocky obstacles that made navigation challenging and obscured radar returns. It was the perfect sanctuary.

The asteroid belt was located roughly between the orbits of Mars and Jupiter. Outside the belt there were numerous irregularly shaped rocky bodies and minor planets and three smaller clusters: the Cybele group, the Hilda family, and the Trojan family. These asteroids were as numerous as those within the asteroid belt and included objects larger than one kilometer wide. Roberts found that the Titans had built in-depth defenses on several asteroids. There were minefields and fortresses with overlapping fields of fire from scores of missile launchers.

The *Warrior* zigzagged from one large asteroid formation to another in short bursts to avoid detection. The Titans could only get a couple of quick returns on radar. They couldn't get anything solid to track. Roberts was relieved when the scanners showed a crevasse in a nearby large asteroid. He was able to establish a charging station for his future operations.

Next, he wanted to build a decryption site on an asteroid, but first he had to locate a Titan junction box. Because of the signals he had detected in the area, he knew there was one nearby.

The asteroid belt with its uncountable deluge of rocks and debris was strewn before him. The ship deployed in a grid search pattern, weaving through the asteroids. Radar and other sensors scanned for any ships that wandered into their path. As the ships advanced, the density of the asteroid field increased, as well as the level of danger. Rocks and dust in the asteroid belt twinkled as they moved across its face.

"Contact, sir. Destroyer bearing 330, mark2."

Roberts muttered. "She may be patrolling this area to protect a communication box. It might be near."

"Should we radio the *Constellation*?"

"No. We'll wait and watch."

Finally, after following the destroyer, Roberts located the junction box. He looked for a nearby location to set up the monitoring and decryption station. He conducted a spiral search looking for an asteroid large enough to hide the site.

They found an innocuous looking rock and designated it Base 83. Although they set up a few weapons on an asteroid, he knew it was scant protection. He directed the construction personally. He sweated even while he descended into the construction spaces. Going from work site to work site, he encouraged the crew and making snap decisions on what to do with the limited supplies. They would have to jury-rig some structures fashioned from scrap.

The engineers unloaded a massive drill-excavator from the ship. It was the size of a tank with tremendous power to drill through the hard iron deposits of the rock. They set about boring a hole one thousand meters straight down, then bore out a series of connected tunnels two meters in diameter. The chamber walls were covered with a sticky gooey sealant that made them airtight. The tunnels connected evacuated chambers that housed the marines and technical staff. One large chamber contained the electrical and computer equipment for the mission. There were other smaller chambers for the oxygen generator, CO_2 scrubber, and electricity generator—everything required to maintain the atmosphere within the site.

The shuttles affixed to the sides of the ship offered not only refuge but temporary quarters for workers. Each party was equipped with tools and parts, but personnel kept shifting between groups, which required coordination. Roberts sent a party of workers to set up a forge and production machine shop on a nearby asteroid to carry out work he didn't want to do aboard the ship. He drove the crew hard, but they responded well. The chiefs were satisfied and beamed with pride. The make-shift dome shape station was cramped and rugged, but it housed the decryption team, their equipment, and a marine detachment. It wasn't much, but it had to do.

Roberts received reports of faint contacts that interrupted their progress several times. But after a week the job was done.

Kate Mahoney said, "Thank you, Captain Roberts. The installation of the quantum computer went well."

Roberts smiled at her bright eager face.

She's so young.

He said, "I hope you have success. Please let me know if you require anything else. The *Warrior* will be leaving soon, but we will remain in the area if you need help."

Kate's green eyes opened wide, and she said, "Can you download the communication files you've collected? I can't wait to get started."

"Certainly."

The next day, striding through the tunnels to the computer chamber Daniel Logan burst into a chamber. His lips were pursed as if they concealed a secret smile. As he swung around the entrance hatch, he ran smack into Kate. Her armload of assorted technology flew into the air and spread across the deck like a fan.

"Sor . . . sorry."

"You should be," she said, her face screwed into a tight scowl. She pointed down and said, "See what you've done?"

She stooped and frantically tried to gather her gear.

"Let me help."

Spying a tablet, she exclaimed, "Oh no! All my work."

Carefully, she tapped the device and waited impatiently until the screen lit up.

"You're just lucky. If that had crashed, I would have . . ."

She balled her fist.

Logan stood there, too startled to speak.

Kate huffed for several more seconds and then said, "Never mind. Let's get to work."

They settled in and made themselves comfortable in the station.

Major James Steward deployed his company of Marines from the 1st Marine Raider Battalion. They provided protection with a few antimissile batteries and rail guns. It wasn't much but it was all the *Warrior* could accommodate. Roberts was confident the base was well hidden. It wasn't likely that the Titan would discover the secret base while Kate and Logan eavesdropped on the Titans. Communications were limited to avoid giving themselves away.

Kate and Logan nicknamed Base 83 "Bletchley Park" and together they began their decryption effort.

Arriving at the outer rings of Saturn, the *Cheshire*, immediately began to collect data and search for targets. One hundred times larger than Earth, the pale-yellow gas giant Saturn is surrounded by 150 moons. Those moons were of special interest to the Titans because of their thin methane atmosphere.

The largest moon, Titan, was over 1.2 million kilometers from the planet. When the sun's ultraviolet radiation struck, it rained liquid methane and produced a methane-rich atmosphere. The United Planets maintained several small mining sites and one small refueling and refitting station in orbit around Titan.

Originally from the red dwarf Gliese-581, located 20.5 light-years away, the Titans wanted Saturn's moons as colonies in the Solar System.

Jaeger surveyed the other moons and found that the second-largest moon, Rhea, also had a tenuous atmosphere. The moons Pandora and Prometheus acted as gravitational influences to confine the planetary rings. The smaller moons, Pan and Atlas, caused waves within those rings. The rings themselves appeared like grooves. The most prominent rings were thick, composed of ice and impurities, with particle sizes ranging from dust to ten meters.

Jaeger was meticulous in watching his ship's wake as it moved through the rings. This was a trick he had learned from Gallant's mission to Saturn.

A good-natured, happy-go-lucky sort of fellow, Charles Jaeger was prone to self-deprecating humor. Crewmembers were often heard laughing out loud in compartments as he passed through. But what made his crew worship him was his pugilistic, give-no-ground aggression.

He had grown up in the heart of Missouri, where tiny communities populated the plains. Small towns dotted the rugged Ozark landscape of hollows. His home sat on a bluff above the Missouri River in the town of Hanging Rock with less than a hundred residents. For the most part, the town still supported small farmers. His parents owned a community hardware store. His mother spent her time raising his four brothers and sisters. When he was growing up, he liked to read adventure stories of epic heroes. He was raised half savage and most people in the town still remember Charles running wild across the countryside. His parents died when he was a teen. He might have fallen into depression, but instead, he hardened and became a resilient, self-reliant officer in the space navy.

The *Cheshire* proceeded according to plan, and Jaeger only caught an occasional glimpse of Titans.

Jaeger assessed the option of using one of the asteroids as a base. The steep ridgelines and cliffs overlapped, affording adequate radar cover from prying enemy eyes. He considered the possibilities. The rocks were all traveling along in rough orbit. They were close enough to be acceptable for his plans.

"This is suitable. We'll maintain a position

within this group."

"Aye aye, sir."

Soon Jaeger was gathering intelligence on the Titan construction on the Saturn moons.

A CIC tech reported, "The Titan military is developing bases."

It wasn't long before he heard.

"Contact! Contact bearing 233, mark 2, range unknown."

Now Jaeger glued his eyes to the radar screen.

"Can you classify it?"

"The return reading is unclear, sir. Could be one large ship or several smaller ships."

"Keep a sharp watch," said Jaeger.

Even this far from the last known enemy position, Jaeger was concerned. Cold, dark empty space held nothing but trouble for the isolated ship. Jaeger paced the deck of his tiny bridge as he tried to reach a decision. If his calculations were off, he would be in trouble. He was eyeing the viewscreen seeking a clue when he heard the crewman.

"It's a destroyer, sir."

"We'll head away from the contact."

Meter by meter, the *Cheshire* crept through the dusty rings careful to avoid a telltale wake.

The Titan destroyer was lying close to his stern. Jaeger looked impatiently at his chronometer. He increased the amplification on his viewscreen to get a better look at the nearby destroyer. He was watching for a sign that he had been detected. So far, none.

Exorbitantly, seconds ticked by.

How far now?

Glancing at the enemy, he was concerned. They were ignoring him and cruising far away. Jager guessed that the enemy was closing in his general direction, but which way should he turn to stay invisible to all of them?

"How much room do we have? How much time?"

He might lose stealth protection while he was near an enemy. He changed course and speed to avoid them.

"The enemy is changing course. We will be coming close to the ship."

He considered his weapons and ability to fight if it came to that. He tensed, awaiting the climactic moment when the enemy would pass.

Jaeger silently cursed the destroyer that was in his way out, but soon the destroyer passed unconcerned.

In just a few days, Captain Charles Jaeger had an extensive picture of the situation. The Titans were shepherding a large transport fleet toward the major moons of Titan and Rhea. Jaeger's assessment was that the Titan fleet was preparing an assault within a few days.

He suggested that the moons be immediately evacuated and sent that information to the *Constellation* which was far away. He warned the local commander as well. But the Saturn squadron was built around two battlecruisers under the command of Admiral Butler who stubbornly refused to hear the bad news and delayed evacuating. That caused serious concerns.

The window for evacuation was rapidly closing.

As a result, Butler was late in beginning evacuation transports and had to make a hasty exit. The Titan were able to close and inflict damage on his squadron. Fortunately, the evacuation transports got away safely.

Jaeger ordered, "Comms, send this message to the *Constellation*, 'Saturn has fallen to the Titan fleet. The Titans are landing major forces from transport to rebuild their presence on the outer planets. Our squadron is fighting an evacuation rearguard action. All will rendezvous with Jupiter squadron.'"

"Aye, aye, sir."

CHAPTER 9

Saturn Falls

The violence of war had changed the world. Melbourne was no longer a happy, adventurous city with people celebrating life. They were fearful and worried, ever wondering if they would have to scurry to an air-raid shelter to protect their lives.

A few weeks after the loss of the Home Fleet, Gallant was working furiously to deal with the ongoing Titan threat. The list of problems that had fallen into Gallant's lap piled up faster than he could solve them. His priority was the security of Earth, but that required standing up more military forces, gathering far-flung units, supporting the outer planets and resupplying their bases, repairing damaged ships and starfighters, recruiting more pilots and soldiers, upgrading production and convoys, feeding civilians, and calming their fears. The list went on.

Luna was the hub of all the Home Fleet's activities, including overhauls and refits. It was an essential base, almost as vital as the Home Fleet itself. It was working overtime at a frantic pace. It meant the difference between repairing and rebuilding their defense or not.

The vibrating hum of the ship's deck touched Gallant's feet. He could take solace in his harmony with the ship and its crew. He was grateful that the stealth recon ships had moved toward the enemy. He felt assured he would get the best information possible. It would allow him to make the best decisions.

The communication officer reported, "Action message, sir. It's from the *Cheshire* about Rear Admiral Butler's command at Saturn station. It's addressed to all units."

Butler's force was the only substantial unit in the outer planets. Gallant was worried about Butler's judgment. Only a week earlier, he had asked Collingsworth to issue a recall order to evacuate Saturn and bring his ships to support Jupiter. But that did not happen.

"Put the action message through to my command console."

The message reported the destruction of the Saturn bases to Titan attack after Butler engaged in a running battle before escaping to Jupiter.

It read:

From: Saturn Squadron
To: All Commands,
Subj: Evacuation of Saturn Station

Ref: (a) Ops Order File 787 (b) Mission Saturn (c) War warring (d) Action report

    1.   Squadron on station in accordance with references (a) and (b)
    2.   Upon receipt ref. (c) assumed defensive posture.
    3.   Upon arrival of Titan fleet began evacuation of station and mining sites.
    4.   Engaged in rear guard battle.
    5.   Attachment ref (d) Action Report.

Benjamin Buford Butler
Rear Admiral Benjamin Buford Butler UPN
Commander Saturn Squadron - UPSS *Behemoth* BC-640

Gallant reviewed the reports and the images of Saturn, and its battle station satellites. It was a battle of fire and ice. A miracle of visual art and hostile violence blended into a cataclysmic symphony. It showed, the squadron's normal disposition and the most likely attack vector of the Titans. He calculated the angle of approach and the missile flight trajectories. In his mind's eye, he could follow the track of hundreds of missiles as the battle must have progressed. His rapid mind was already dealing with the fallout. He envisioned how the Saturn fleet would have been outgunned and how Butler would have found himself completely helpless.

There was no hope for a significant counterattack or even any expectation that surviving ships would escape the follow-up salvos. Gallant began calculating the distance of his forces and the remaining bases. There were decisions to be made about repositioning the remaining assets. The leverage the Titans had gained through this battle was enormous.

Gallant wished to rescue the situation with a sortie into the area but realized that was not possible. He sustained himself by looking for survivors.

"Send a message to *Cheshire* to swing through the sector and pick up any escape pods."

"Perhaps . . ." Fletcher began.

No one in his right senses would expect more from him at this time, but Fletcher asked, "Are we going to send a rescue mission for the survivors, sir?"

"That is not an option, XO. We'll have to trust that the evacuation to Jupiter was complete."

The OOD looked up from the message and searched Gallant's face before he too could see the reality of the situation.

"Sir, we have a brief supplemental message from *Cheshire*. It only states, 'We've found something.' Then communications go dead, sir."

CHAPTER 10

Without Reflection

Gallant frowned at his distorted reflection on the glossy steel-and-glass senate building in the heart of Melbourne. Setting his jaw, he pushed open the heavy doors with nervous anticipation. Inside, the embedded sensors scanned his ID pin, and a security guard passed him through. He had only gone a few steps before Captain Julie Anne McCall caught him.

"I've been waiting for you. This way," she said as she ushered him into the hearing chamber.

As he entered the auditorium, Gallant was taken aback by the austere gathering of powerful people. He immediately recognized the key figures of the senate's armed services oversight committee. Several of Neumann's political allies joined them in the front row. There was also a plethora of media reporters. He guessed that his interview was going to be broadcast, and President Neumann would be watching.

A recent series of ominous Titan attacks had heightened public fear, causing the senators to look sterner and more unforgiving than usual. They sat in the ornate hall surrounded by statues and paintings of distinguished government leaders. None of the adornments was shiny or bright. The overall effect was rather dull, grey, and depressing.

"Don't look so worried," said McCall. "You've got friends." She pointed to the back of the auditorium where Admiral Collingsworth looked impressive. Then he saw Alaina behind the admiral, and he smiled. She brightened his day.

Gallant took his place at the focal point in front of nine senators. He remained at attention, shifting his weight uneasily.

"Please take your seat and make yourself comfortable, Captain Gallant," said Senator Griffin. He turned and gave the television cameras a flamboyant grin. He was the committee chairman presiding over the investigation. Behind him were several staffers and behind them were several rows of reporters and other media personalities. At the very back of the packed room was a line of military officers.

Gallant sat down on the uncomfortable hardwood chair and moved it closer to the table. He took a sip from a glass of water to quench his parched throat.

This is all too familiar, he thought.

Griffin said, "This is an armed services oversight review of the military actions and security efforts since the vicious Titan attack on November 30.

This will be a fact-finding inquiry into the recent military actions in the asteroid belt and around Saturn. We welcome your testimony before this committee."

He paused and his expression became somber as he said, "Our goal is to extract accountability for the current conduct of the war."

The audience voiced its approval with shouts of "Here, here!" and stomping of feet.

Griffin continued, "Each senator will provide a written copy of their conclusions for the transcript. This hearing will be video recorded, and an unclassified edited version of these proceedings may be released to the public."

The audience remained restless, and more shouts erupted.

Griffin banged his gavel several times to restore order. "The audience will remain quiet and respectful, or I will be forced to clear the room."

The crowd simmered down.

Griffin began his opening statement. "The central pillar of our democratic governance has been the building of an empire through free trade amongst the many worlds of our solar system and colonial stars. This is being accomplished under the aegis of the United Planets authority. Our foreign policy establishment believes not only that this strategy offers the best way to secure our interests but that it represents humanity's best hope for long-term survival. Yet, in the era of nuclear weapons and faster-than-light travel, our entire species now faces the threat of great alien powers. These are stark facts and powerful fears."

Griffin's eyes swept the room. "This committee will leave no stone unturned in uncovering the truth about the performance of our military during the latest developments of this conflict."

This wasn't a conventional predicament. The debacle created a crisis of belief in government and military credibility. The people expected that that the government wouldn't be blindsided by a military fiasco. Those who perceived that they were losing the war knew there would be instability at home even as they failed to master events. Stopping the erosion of credibility in the short term would require the Neumann administration to clean up its mess. Once the immediate difficulty was past, the real work of rethinking the military organization would take place. Then he gazed at Gallant and said, "Let's start with the failure to defend Saturn. Tell us, did the enemy gain bases on the outer planets?""

Gallant chose his words carefully. "They were secretive and powerful, sir. The solar system is large and couldn't oppose them at every point at this time. Circumstances are now changing, and we hope to be able to dislodge the Titans sometime in the future."

Step by step, Griffin took Gallant through *Cheshire's* report of the Titan invasion followed by Butler's evacuation. The court and the audience listened intently.

"Senator, we had limited resources," said Gallant.

"Really?" said one Senator, speaking out of turn

with a tinge of doubt in his voice. "The fall of Saturn and the chaotic withdrawal have been seen as a disaster across the worlds. Nowhere has the perception of weakness been more trumpeted than in the media, where outlets run predictions of our national decline."

Griffin said, "We must take immediate steps to deter the Titans from invading more of our system. They should find it hard to mount a difficult landing and sustain a prolonged counterinsurgency—both of which could produce significant casualties for them. First, we should provide our bases with significant quantities of the anti-ship weapon, the Goliath missile. Second, we should acquire advanced mine technology. Third, we need to increase military units stationed there."

A pained atmosphere descended over the room.

"Our forces are bound by the president's orders to minimize, at all costs, the threat to Earth. The Titans made abundantly clear…that they were going to exploit any weakness that appeared," said Gallant.

"Perhaps." Griffin's tone had a distinctive animus. "But this report is a disgrace. You left vital population areas vulnerable."

Gallant said, "The withdrawal was expedited but, in the end, an extraordinary effort to evacuate Saturn was required. I sent repeated messages urging them to prepare and leave. There were citizens who were reluctant to give up their life's work."

"Did you take an appropriate risk, or were you

reckless with Earth's safety, Mr. Gallant?"

"I took the appropriate risk, sir," said Gallant.

"Did you get admiralty authorization for the strategy you employed for the asteroid belt?"

"No, sir," answered Gallant.

"Did you withhold information from the admiralty?"

"No, sir! They received full reports."

Gallant's cheeks turned bright red.

"Really? I am amazed to hear that. Most senators do not appreciate your tone-deaf defense of your actions. You act as if you've made no mistakes," said Griffin. "There has been an effort by the military to pat yourselves on the back for what little success you've had."

The oversight committee neglected to discuss the changes in the administration. The most high-profile change was secretary of defense, who was moved aside following media criticism over the hasty planning for the evacuation from Saturn.

Gallant said, "The problems facing our world are more acute and urgent. The resources to address them have diminished."

The tension mounted. With each inquiry, it became clear that Gallant was being investigated. He could lose his command which he feared could lead to strategic blunders by the admiralty.

Chairman Griffin turned and said, "I yield the floor to Senator Markey for initial questioning."

Senator Markey said, "The imperative of protecting trade lanes between the planets is threatened by the enemy. These are essential and must be protected. Supply-chain disruptions will make everything more expensive for consumers. Bottlenecks at ports as well as congestion at terminals, warehouses and distribution networks have extended the time it takes to obtain goods. How are you addressing the Titan threat to our free trade? What provisions have you made to ensure convoy safety?"

"From a security perspective, we have a conundrum," said Gallant. "Our supply chains span multiple planets and multiple stars. Keeping them secure requires considerable military force. Much of our available force is tied to naval primacy around Earth. That effectively means," as Gallant put it, "that the navy can only secure a limited flow of trade in goods and energy."

"One of our lessons is that while we are very effective in dealing with fleet threats, raiding squadrons are troubling," he went on. "An additional complication is that the new genetic engineering laws are intolerant and limiting those being accepted into the armed forces."

"The genetic laws are not up for discussion here. That is a legislative matter," said Griffin. "Our concern is you. What is your personal responsibility for the Saturn disaster?"

For a moment, Gallant sought refuge in a faraway mirage as his gaze fell on the dancing mosaic of the colors swirling in his water glass.

Pounding his gavel, Griffin said, "Sir, I asked you a question. Will you not respond?"

"Senator," said Gallant looking up. "Will you repeat the question?"

"I don't understand how you can make such disastrous mistakes that put the rest of us at risk."

Gallant reflected, "Senator, perhaps your understanding would be better if you yourself had served in the armed forces."

"One more comment like that and I will hold you in contempt!"

After the hearing, Gallant was asked to meet President Neumann in his office at the capital.

A rugged-faced marine stood at rigid attention outside the President's luxury suite. Its opulent carpet, vaulted ceilings, and antique furnishings were on display. A side door opened, and another marine escorted Gallant into the president's private office.

President Gerome Neumann appeared not to just tower over but to completely preside over his rosewood desk. He was tall, fit, and still young-looking for his years in his perfectly tailored suit. His youthful face and physique, the product of Earth's finest genetic engineering, created a dominating presence.

At first glance, the sanctuary lacked any intimate personal possessions. There were no memorabilia, trinkets, or photos of his wife and family. The viewscreen was filled with statistical data of Neumann's personal financial empire.

"Come in," said the President politely, holding back his normally acerbic tongue. He waved Gallant to a chair.

"Have a seat. You and I have a lot of history, but circumstances demand that we put that aside for the good of the planet. Do you agree?"

Gallant waited for his emotions to catch up with what his mind already knew. Neumann had intended to make him pay for his lack of submission. He undoubtedly wanted to remove Gallant from command.

Neumann had claimed that the surprise attack had been beaten off with reasonable losses. He highlighted the arrival of additional space fleet forces and of Task Force 34. It was designed to have a calming and reassuring effect on the public.

Gallant was unhappy with the deception. He felt a forthright appeal to the public would foster unified support for the fleet. He thought of the rugged individualists who colonized the outer planets and how tough and solid they had been through adversity. Those early pioneers were followed by descendants eager to travel to the stars.

Central to all deliberations was who was to lead the military operations in the solar system and what place Captain Gallant had. President Neumann and the admiralty considered replacing Gallant. He was a Natural, which was the antithesis to Neumann's genetic engineering laws and his central thesis. But Gallant had the only successful fighting force available. This was an awkward position for Neumann. To reestablish his credibility, he was being forced to support a person he wanted to remove.

The president said, "I'm afraid this is going to be a long war. There are two prominent strategies for our people if we are to pursue empire building. One option is to reduce our footprint in the stars with little regard for multilateral institutions or free trade. As we withdraw, a natural balance of power could emerge. Each colony could take responsibility for its own defense. We could then concentrate on human development through genetic enhancements. The alternative is to form alliances and build greater security through an active presence in key theaters of space."

"I take it that you would prefer the former," said Gallant. "Have you considered an alliance with the Chameleon? They have more technology that we could benefit from. That would eventually allow us to conduct faster, stealthier ships. Such a partnership would be about advancing our strategic interests, upholding a rules-based order, and promoting peace and stability."

Neumann frowned. "The consensus supporting an interstellar order seems to be fading as geopolitical challenges rise from aliens like the Titans and the Chameleon. Whether anyone can sustain a realistic strategy that works remains to be seen. Inadequate responses to the complex challenges facing us will leave us in peril. Even as we steel ourselves for these struggles, we should recognize that dark and dangerous times are ahead."

Gallant sighed. *More failures seem likely.*

Neumann said, "The Titans are a hard people to figure out. You made a reconnaissance mission to their home world. What're they really like?"

Gallant said, "They're a highly intelligent product of genetic engineering."

"Failed genetic engineering," said Neumann. "Not comparable to how we are handling the technology." He leaned forward intently, "We won't fall into those problems. I've plans for our benefit."

"You sound as if any genetic compromise is possible without problems."

"Not impossible, given our history and character."

Gallant said, "The Titan's emphasis is on their strict code of obedience, that led to the privation of the Titan people. It is a clear illustration of the hazards of such experiments. I'd hate for us to follow their poor example."

Neumann said, "Don't lecture me on the perils of genetic engineering. It is a boon to mankind."

"Natural selection offers opportunities you can't predict. Me, for instance."

"Ha! You are one of a kind," said Neumann dismissively. "Your unique talents will die when you die!"

CHAPTER 11

Sortie

Gallant met with Commander Margret Fletcher in the captain's cabin while the *Constellation* was on station near the moon. Their blank unblinking stares were fixed on a very long list of equipment breakdowns and needed repairs. Although the *Constellation* and its space wing were operational, their efficiency was far below their past capability.

The XO said, "Captain, the many tasks that I had hoped we would finish in refit have been on hold and we must make some band-aid patches to keep things running smoothly."

"I know, Commander, but even if there were room in any of the overwhelmed shipyards, there still isn't a chance of the *Constellation* going in for refit. She's essential to the defense of Earth. She can't be spared. It's impossible."

"Even a two-week refit could accomplish so much. I'm begging for an opportunity to return this ship to her appropriate place as head of the fleet."

Gallant sighed. "You're right of course, but it is not possible, XO. You'll will simply have to go on fashioning your MacGyver talents to keep this bucket of bolts together.

He cracked a smile and hoped she would relent and smile as well, but her frown was frozen.

A buzzer sounded from Gallant's desk.

"Speak."

"Captain, action message from the *Warrior*," said the CIC operator.

"Patch it through to my cabin."

"Aye, aye, sir."

A minute later, Gallant and Fletcher were pouring over the news.

Gallant read:

> From: *Warrior*
> To: *Constellation*
> Contact Alert!
> Enemy battlecruiser and escorts on intercept course with convoy 2421.
> Intercept in twelve hours.
> Position coordinates: 34.567 555.44
> *Captain John Roberts*

Gallant pulled up his computer plot and fed the data into it.

Fletched said, "That enemy squadron intends to raid an important convoy."

Gallant precisely calculated that the most likely point of intercept.

"See, this is why the *Constellation* must be available at all times."

"Sir?"

"We can take advantage of this sighting by the *Warrior*."

"Surely you don't intend to take the task force away from Earth to intercept this lone enemy squadron. That could be exactly what the Titans want. It could be a decoy."

"No. Not the task force, but perhaps a small strike element. The distance is short, and we can strike and return quickly."

He decided that a swift *Constellation* foray with only a light destroyer escort could intercept this squadron as it poised to hit the convoy. He gambled he could leave the defense of Earth to its remaining forces.

He navigated a precise orbit to reach a launch point for his starfighters and sent them to strike.

His gamble paid off.

The entire action was brief, decisive, and satisfying. But when Gallant sat down to write the action report, he found it difficult to put the event into its proper perspective. It was a victory to be sure, but it would have little consequence to the war. In fact, it was merely a minor skirmish.

However, the news media got advanced disclosure of the success from the president's office and a fuss was being made. So, he thought he ought to pen a few pithy words into an after-action report though he doubted he would like its results. He pulled out the ship's log and reviewed the short entries.

His after-action report was appropriately brief. It read, "The *Constellation* destroyed one enemy battle-cruiser and several destroyers to safeguard convoy 2421. The *Constellation* and its escort returned to Earth safely without loss and with minimal damage."

He added an addendum detailing the damage suffered to a few starfighters. As an afterthought, he included the expenditure of ammunition that would have to be replaced.

Naively, Gallant thought that that would be the end of the matter. It was after all, a relatively minor scuffle compared to the many large engagements he had faced before.

But the convoy crews had witnessed the action and were overjoyed at their salvation. When they reached port, they were flooded by the news media. It was the first glimmer of good news to report in sometime and it was given tremendous coverage. The action was heralded as a heroic triumph and became front page news for days. Interviews with members of the convoy crews went viral.

For the very first time, the public got a comprehensive picture of who Henry Gallant was and what the *Constellation* had accomplished.

CHAPTER 12

Promotion

Gallant worked in his cabin on the *Constellation* while it orbited Earth. He was trying to develop an action plan for redeploying his ships. Rubbing his forehead, he struggled to find the proper distribution of starfighters and the resources he needed for his depleted force.

A knock caused him to look up from his overloaded desk. "Enter."

McCall opened the door looking like a cat that just swallowed a canary.

Gallant said, "Well, I hope that expression means you have some good news."

"I do," she said proudly. She took a step forward but was forced to stop and take stock of the tiny room.

It was small, sparse, and could have used a coat of paint. The only thing hanging on the wall was a computer screen. Several overloaded shelves sagged with computer printouts, documents, and miscellaneous devices. The cot was covered with books and graphical output. The disarray extended to the deck, which had repair parts and various other paraphernalia scattered about. It was clear that the usually tidy occupant had slacked off.

Frowning, McCall was forced to step into the space like a soldier hazarding a minefield. Each step was judiciously placed, yet she still heard a crunch and knocked over a pile of documents. Finally, arriving at Gallant's desk, she was able to extend her hand.

"What's this?" he asked, taking the communique. He read through the letter twice before he understood that the message was an order authorizing his promotion to rear admiral, effective upon receipt.

It was accompanied by a personal letter from Admiral Collingsworth.

> My Dear Henry Gallant,
>
> It is with relish that I take this opportunity to update you on the latest news. Thanks to your good services, I was able to reassume my duties as fleet admiral and undertake the defense of Earth. I have begun detailing the work that must be done to supply your task force. Unfortunately, I must inform you of more bad news from the outer planets. Jupiter Station has fallen, and reports of Titan reoccupation of Saturn's moon have been confirmed. You will shortly receive official notification of these events in greater detail, I'm sure.

On a positive and more personal side, I would like to congratulate you on your promotion to rear admiral. It is well deserved. You will receive the official notification.

I have sent with this message via Commander Whittingham, whom I hope you accept as your chief of staff. He will prove invaluable in assembling the staff for your new position. I believe you can trust him in all things and that he will serve you as well as he has served me.

Yours very faithfully,
George Forsyth Collingsworth
Admiral George Forsyth Collingsworth

P.S. Commander Carter Whittingham will aid in facilitating our private communication.

P.S.S. If you can be tempted out of your ship, Edith and I would enjoy the company of you and Alaina for dinner this evening. It seems a small celebration would be appropriate.

"Ha, h'm," muttered Gallant.

"Ha, h'm," repeated McCall giggling.

"Huh?" Gallant blushed. For the first time, he realized that someone else was aware of his tendency to use this idiom as a procrastinating device when he was at a loss for words.

McCall suppressed her mirth and said, in a more serious tone, "Congratulations, Admiral."

"I wasn't expecting this," he muttered, brushing aside a lock of his brown hair from his forehead.

"Why not? You earned it."

While he was aware that Admiral Collingsworth had recommended him, flag officer promotions required President Neumann's approval. So, he had discounted the possibility.

Collingsworth wanted this for the good of the service, but what was Neumann's aim?

While Gallant believed in duty, honor, and service, the motivations of politicians were often obscure to him. However, he had recently come to appreciate their convoluted contortions in reasoning to their advantage. By praising, extolling, and glorifying Gallant's accomplishment, Neumann identified himself as the power behind his triumphal victory. The adulation of the success suggested that it was Neumann's backing, training, and planning that had inspired the achievement. And that he was magnanimously sharing credit with Gallant.

In any case, the promotion would be useful to Gallant. Not only would it give him more authority when dealing with reluctant civilian leaders in shipping and manufacturing, but he could look forward to twisting the arms of a few shipyard supervisors. They had been a particular thorn in his side over the years.

"Commander Whittingham?" asked Gallant.

"He's waiting outside."

Carter Whittingham was as tall as Gallant and

though he was balding, he had an erudite face and proud bearing.

"I'm glad to meet you, Commander."

Whittingham looked respectful but he raised his eyebrow quizzically.

"Yes, sir," said the commander, handing Gallant a copy of his personnel record.

Gallant took the folder and placed it in his lap without looking at it. "Tell me about yourself. Tell me what is not in this folder."

"I'm married to the love of my life. I have a ten-year-old daughter and I would wrestle a grizzle bear just to entertain her. They are my life, and I would give my life for them if need be. And I believe that to be the case today."

"Well said, Commander. I shall need help building a staff for a new formation made primarily out of Task Force 34 but supplemented by whatever stray ship we can gather from the inner planets. There will be a great deal of administration and organizational duties. Are you up to the task?"

"You'll not find me wanting, sir."

"And did Admiral Collingsworth have anything else to offer?"

The commander looked at Gallant and around the cabin. "Yes, sir. The admiral briefed me on some details that were too sensitive to include in the message."

"What are they?" asked Gallant. He was surprised by the candid response but listened to the personal message being conveyed.

That evening, the marine that escorted Gallant and Alaina through the Collingsworth's estate kept his eye's "in-the-boat" and maintained a meticulously professional expression. They, however, gawked when they entered the living quarters.

While Gallant appreciated Alaina's achievement in decorating their apartment on a meager living allowance, this extravagant home was beyond comparison. They stepped on a carpet so rich and thick that they sank into it. The living room was so spacious that it could have held their entire one-bedroom apartment.

The furniture was cleverly arranged for both comfort and style. A trophy cabinet stood against one wall. It displayed a plethora of awards and prestigious photographs that the many years of military service had produced. The images showed the admiral with distinguished leaders from many walks of life. Not to be overshadowed, Ms. Collingsworth was also well represented through her many charity roles and public service positions.

"Admiral and Ms. Gallant," announced the marine.

"I'm delighted, genuinely delighted, you could come," said Edith Collingsworth, smiling broadly and extending her hands. "I've enjoyed visits from Alaina over the last few months, and I am finally meeting the man she talks endlessly about."

Gallant produced a crooked smile. He was unaware that Alaina and Ms. Collingsworth were even acquainted. Alaina had never mentioned it.

"Let me introduce you to our other guests. This is Commander and Ms. Whittingham, Carter and Sylvia."

Soon it was dinner time, and they arranged themselves around a lavish table.

"An excellent table," commented Ms. Whittingham.

When the wine was poured, Collingsworth rose and said, "Let us raise a glass in toast of the United Planets' newest admiral, Henry Gallant."

The celebration of his promotion was toasted several more times and congratulations were readily offered.

The dinner was a roast with vegetables steaming with butter and freshly baked bread. A delicious sugary dessert followed, and an after-dinner drink.

Soon they were relaxing in the living room. The admiral lowered himself into a comfy chair, and his guests did likewise.

Alaina asked Edith about her family of three boys and two girls. Each offspring now had a family of their own. They stayed connected. There were grandchildren as well. The family portraits were brought out, and some funny stories were recalled.

Ms. Whittingham regaled the table with the hair-raising adventures of her four-year-old boy, Benjamin. He was the terror of the neighborhood. Everyone laughed gayly.

Ms. Whittingham asked Alaina, "Do you have children?"

"No. Not yet," she said with a wistful sigh.

Ms. Whittingham smiled broadly and said, "Not to worry. You're young and your time will come."

"I'm sure it will," said Alaina casting her eyes on Gallant.

He blushed but said nothing.

The dinner discussion turned to complements for Gallant's accomplishments and promotion.

Alaina's pleasure for her husband's accolades was evident, but Gallant detected a reserve when she looked his way.

Edith said, "I'm sure you've been intrigued by your wife's wonderful adventures as an award-winning journalist for the Metropolis news media."

"Award-winning?" Gallant was instantly guilty. In the excitement of events and his homecoming, he had completely neglected to inquire about Alaina's work as a news media journalist.

"She has almost single-handedly moved mountains about the genetic engineering laws. As the wife of one of the most famous naturals, she has pushed the topic into public attention. She was relentless in publishing article after article stirring up public support and interviewing everyone under the sun."

Gallant looked stunned.

"Did Alaina tell you about our rally last month at the open forum with the President after he made his speech at the university?"

"Huh?" he said, drawing in a sharp breath.

"Oh."

"Alaina stood up and challenged the administration's performance. Do you know what the President said to shut her up?"

Gallant shook his head.

"He said, 'Do you think the public hears your squeaky little voice?'"

There was an audible gasp in the room.

"And do you know how your wife responded?" continued Edith.

Gallant looked at his wife.

"She came right back here and began plotting on how to amplify that voice," said Edith. "Together, we are leading a petition drive to get a voter initiative on the next congressional ballot. It will rescind the genetic engineering laws that restrict naturals. Alaina has also been writing editorials on how discriminating against naturals hurts our nation and our military forces. And she and I are forming a committee to get the vote out for this November's election."

The evening continued in a festive, comfortable manner until late into the night. But when they left, Gallant looked at Alaina with new eyes.

CHAPTER 13

Defeat is an Orphan

Rear Admiral Henry Gallant climbed the stairs to the fleet headquarters building in Melbourne. On his right was Commander Carter Whittingham, his chief of staff. On his left was Captain Margret Fletcher, the newly appointed captain of the Constellation.

Fleet headquarters housed the admiralty command staff of the space navy. Designed by an Australian architect, it resided alongside the Yarra River. The imposing structure was considered a modern masterpiece. Senior officers thrived behind its many layers of impenetrable security in a huge building complex.

As Gallant entered, a security guard scanned his comm pin and opened the door into the main conference room. He was greeted by a familiar voice.

"Hello, Henry," said Admiral Collingsworth. "Delighted to see you. Let me introduce you to the flag officers present. Please stop me if you already know them."

Gallant shook hands with the half-dozen flag officers and the group took their seats around a large table.

After the destruction of the Home Fleet, Gallant discovered that never was an aphorism more appropriate than "Victory has a thousand fathers, but defeat is an orphan." Even before Earth was safe, political, military, and social organizations had mobilized to lay blame. That blame would have most certainly fallen at Admiral Graves' feet if he were alive, but his death left those angered without a target. Many of the senior officers present were anxious to avoid any blame being cast in their direction.

Collingsworth said, "It's been a month, and now the entire war has been transformed. The Titans have complete control of Saturn's moon, and they are building more bases. Convoys from Gliese-beta have brought new colonists to populate them. So, they have begun turning their attention to strangling our supply lines by attacking convoys and key bases."

One officer said, "The evacuation operation from outlying sites is taking place under perilous conditions. Military personnel and essential equipment was loaded onto the final departing planes. The Embassy issued a security alert which said unessential personnel should leave. The military is evacuating using all available units even as the window begins to close. A disparate group of veterans, military contractors, and aid workers struggled to get as many people off Jupiter's moons as they could before the window is shut by the aliens."

Another officer said, "This disaster has revealed grave structural weaknesses of our current political leadership. If these habits don't change, there will be more debacles in the future. This crisis has revealed a presidential administration with little understanding of military problems."

There were some nods and several shaking heads at such a controversial comment.

Collingsworth said, "Let me offer some good news. Task Force 47 has returned from the Dog Star, Sirius. Though it has only the *Yorktown* CVS-642 and one battlecruiser, it is a welcomed addition. I intend to shift my flag to the *Yorktown* and make it my flagship."

He added, "Let me begin by briefing you on our current risk assessment. We have multiple risks, the safety of our people on wide flung planets and bases. The export of food and finished goods from Earth and the import of raw materials and supply parts to Earth are needed to maintain the war machine."

One officer asked, "How can we deal with the threats?"

Collingsworth said, "I propose forming Task Force 47 as the center of a new Home Fleet. That will allow more freedom of action for Task Force 34."

Gallant's pleasure at the proposal was dashed when Collingsworth added, "However, Admiral Gallant, your freedom comes at a price. You will transfer carrier *Courageous* and battlecruiser *Invincible* to Task Force 47. That will ensure sufficient strength for rebuilding the Home Fleet."

Gallant considered objecting to the loss of two mainstays of his task force, but he quickly calculated that Collingsworth's solution was the most practical. He hoped more far-flung ships would come home soon.

"I have some more bad news for you, I fear," said Collingsworth, his mouth turned down.

Gallant reframed from asking, "What is it?" Instead, he sat even more straight at attention.

"There is an immediate assignment for Task Force 34 to carry out."

"Yes, Admiral?" asked Gallant, awaiting clarification.

"There is a convoy of particular importance that needs an escort, and there is none available other than your force to protect it."

Gallant wanted to take his few ships and seek the Titan battle fleet. Instead, he bit his lip and said, "I see, sir."

"The fact of the matter is that the president has personally made this request."

Neumann is nefariously safeguarding his wealth. He is prioritizing the safety of his personal mining interests.

"It is for this highest reason of state that we have levied this requirement on you."

Gallant grimaced. "I find it hard to believe that this decision was appropriately prioritized."

For a moment, several admirals at the table looked astonished at the effrontery of a more junior officer to challenge the president's judgment.

It took several minutes for tempers to cool enough for Gallant to continue. "I have only a very few ships to accomplish many impossible tasks. You must agree that there are many necessities beyond this to deal with."

A clearly unhappy Collingsworth said, "There are, as you point out many concerns that must be dealt with. I advised against this particular operation, but I was personally overruled by the president."

Gallant often felt that chances often came in threes. Like wishes, once you take a chance, they can't be undone or reimagined. So, it's better to think carefully before acting. No matter how attractive the chance may appear to be. And oh, by the way, don't count on the next chance occurring any time soon. For now, he had a chance of operating the reduced Task Force 34 with some independence and this initial assignment was clearly not negotiable.

So, he said, "I understand, sir."

"I am not specifying which ships you must dispatch. I will leave the details to you," said Collingsworth.

"Thank you, sir. I am aware of the pressures upon your command. What are your orders, sir?"

Collingsworth frowned as he handed Gallant the written orders.

Even though Gallant was the most junior flag officer there, he commanded the only mobile forces left in the system. Several of the senior officers present voiced support for the orders. Lots of them wanted to be in charge. The best and brightest officers had died with the Home Fleet. Those remaining were anxious for promotion, and Gallant was in their way.

CHAPTER 14

Doors

Ensign Daniel Logan slammed shut the computer room door located deep in the bowels of the Bletchley Park asteroid.

SPRAT! CRACKLE!

He jumped. "What was that?!"

Forensic xenoarchaeologist Kate Mahoney said, "Network issues. I haven't ironed out all the bugs in the quantum computer interface, yet. Don't worry, I'll get there."

"Does that happen often?"

"Not so much. But the equipment is delicate and sensitive to disturbing vibrations from things like doors."

"Doors?"

"You know about doors, don't you?" asked Kate.

Daniel Logan's blank stare told her he didn't. But he was often at a loss when responding to the young woman. They had worked together for nearly a year in the Ross system, and she was still a complete mystery to him. However, the fact that they had somehow managed to find keys to the critical three puzzles that led to the destruction of the Great Ship was worth remembering.

She said, "Doors are the demarcation between the known and the unknown. Open a door, and all the secrets behind it are revealed."

Logan's blank stare didn't change.

Kate sighed. "When I was six, I wanted to understand what hieroglyphics meant. I had seen some in a book describing ancient Egypt. I was fascinated by a language I hadn't learned."

"How many languages did you know by age six?" asked Logan snidely, expecting the answer to be one.

To his surprise, Kate said, "Seven."

"Seven?" he gasped. "Really?"

She added, "Well, to be honest, I was only proficiently in six. I was still struggling with written Chinese. In fact, it was the nature of Chinese characters that drew my attention to hieroglyphics."

Chagrined at Kate's prodigious ability, Logan asked, "You were reading hieroglyphics at six years old?"

"Don't be silly. Of course, not. I can't say that I was actually reading hieroglyphics until I was seven. It took me nearly a year because I didn't know about the Rosetta Stone until I was well along in my effort."

"Oh."

"Imagine my amazement when I saw a copy

of that translation artifact. It was a magnificent moment in my life." Kate tapped Logan on his forehead and added, "A door opened for me."

Logan's mouth hung open,

"You still don't get doors, do you?"

"Yeah," said Logan sheepishly. "I get your message, but I don't know if we speak the same language."

Suddenly, a scowl flashed across her face, but it was quickly dismissed.

"Oh! The same language, how exciting. That would be wonderful. But even if we spoke the same language, can I trust you to speak the truth?"

Logan furrowed his brow. "Do you doubt my sincerity?"

Kate said, "Communication is tricky. People are always guessing at intent and nuance, but they often miss deeper meaning."

Logan said, "I'm glad to learn how confident you are in your language skills. Our new assignment will require them. Captain Gallant expects us to break the new Titan secret communications code. That's why he suggested we name this site, Bletchley Park after a previous code breaker's laboratory."

Kate considered what lay ahead of them. She was still uncomfortable in her new surroundings. They had been dropped off in the middle of the asteroid field. Captain Roberts had constructed the isolated military base in the rocky terrain of the twenty-kilometer-thick asteroid. But the asteroid was close to a Titan communication junction box which the *Warrior* monitored and tapped.

She appreciated the quantum computer that Roberts had installed. A small SIA technical support team and one company of Major James Steward's marines provided support. Roberts was confident the Titans wouldn't discover this secret base while the team eavesdropped on them.

Kate said, "Captain Gallant broke the Titan code years ago when he tapped into the Titan communication network. He's been intercepting many of their orders ever since. Does he really need us?"

"The Titans upgraded with the Chameleon technology," said Logan. "Besides taking their stealth ability, they also integrated the Chameleon encryption code into their network. It's a whole new thing. Captain Gallant has been stumped. It's our job to break the new code."

"The Chameleon communicate using an AI chip in their brain. Can you guess how an encrypted form of AI chip technology can be married into a Titan top-secret network?"

Logan looked chagrined. "No, I can't, but I'm surprised to hear of your reluctance. I would have thought you would jump at a chance to show how easily you could add a new language to your legendary skill set."

Kate's red cheeks glowed with rising anger.

Logan took a step back. "Well? Do you want to back out?"

"Of course not."

"Then how do we start? Do you have any suggestions?"

Kate sat down and crossed her arms. She was still simmering from his "legendary skill set" remark.

Logan sat across the table from her and waited, saying nothing.

Finally, Kate said, "OK."

She stood up and began pacing the room. "Instead of guessing how to decrypt this complex concoction, let's reverse engineer it. Consider how we would build a new encryption secret code if we were the Titans, and the Chameleon technology fell into our lap."

Logan said, "Hey. That's a good idea. We can work backward."

Kate grimaced. "It's not backward to start at the beginning of their development process."

"You know what I mean. But even doing that, wouldn't the Titans build a super complicated code using two languages and two AI technologies."

"Not necessarily. Think for a moment as if you were the Titan encryption expert who spent his life perfecting his own code that he believed was awesome."

"Yeah. He wouldn't want to just throw that away. He would keep as much as possible and add the Chameleon technology to it."

"Exactly," said Kate slapping her hand on the table. "That means we already know a great deal."

"We do?"

"We know the Titan language and their encryption techniques, as well as the Chameleon language. That leaves only one additional layer to discover, the Chameleon AI interface."

"Why do you think they just added a single layer rather than integrating the technology throughout?"

"Think about it. You want a communication network that can rapidly process signals. If you make the code unnecessarily complex, the processing time becomes prohibitive."

Kate looked at Logan for a second and then added, "They would add only as much new technology as they felt would guarantee security without sacrificing efficiency. You know how the Titans like efficiency?"

Logan nodded. "I can see your logic. It makes sense. But that still leaves a completely new technology to unravel."

Balling her fists, she said, "Daniel, really. We re-engineered much of the Chameleon technology while we were in the Ross system. We're probably nearly as good as their engineers by now. We can beat this AI tech."

Something in Logan's eyes shifted.

She stepped toward the door in the room. As she twisted the knob, she fixed Logan with a stare. "We're going to break that code before . . . well faster than you think."

With that, Kate stepped through the door and was gone, but she left behind a lingering air of promise.

CHAPTER 15

Cat and Mouse

Henry Gallant stopped short when a voice asked, "Can I be of help, Admiral?"

He blinked twice before he realized he was at the entrance to the captain's cabin.

He muttered, "Ha, h'm," and stood still for a moment.

Flustered, he tried to recover his poise by asking, "Are . . . you . . . settled in yet?"

Captain Margret Fletcher said, "Yes, thank you, Admiral. This is a giant step up from by XO quarters. I'm still not used to it." She chuckled, "Do you know that this morning, I actually stumbled into my old cabin by mistake?"

"Ha. I can see how that could happen." Awkwardly, he turned and retraced his steps. He took the alternate passage to the admiral's stateroom, all the while muttering to himself.

Aboard the *Constellation*, the admiral had his

own bridge called the flag bridge. It was where he was stationed during battle. The admiral commanded the task force from there, while the captain was still responsible for command of the ship from the ship's bridge.

The flag officer area opened into a plush lounge with an enormous couch. An adjacent office area called the war room was where the staff received orders and carried out fleet communications. The next room is the tactical command and control center for the flag operations. It was stuffed with sensors, computers, and communication gear for directing the fleet operations. This center was separate from *Constellation's* CIC, which directed the individual ship. Finally, there was a hatch that led to the admiral's personal quarters.

When Gallant reached his destination, a marine at the entrance gave him a sharp salute and opened the door.

Waiting for him were Captain Fletcher, and Commander Whittingham and his staff. The conference table and viewscreens were alive with information for a detailed briefing.

Gallant was impressed with Whittingham's initiative.

He said, "Open a holographic video conference for the senior commanding officers."

"Aye aye, sir."

Whittingham opened a channel and said, "The senior commanding officers are present online."

Gallant looked at the life-sized three-dimensional holographic images of each officer. He saw experienced faces.

There was Captain Donahue of the *Indefatigable*. He had long, sable hair, high cheekbones, and round black eyes. He was a commanding figure. Captain Hernandez of the *Invincible* was next. A muscular, lanky man with eyes that gleamed. He sported a full mustache. Then came Captain Jackson of the *Courageous* was a middle-aged woman with a withering stare and chiseled features.

The senior officers looked eager to hear about future operations.

Gallant welcomed the officers and then said, "Our immediate problem is to keep Earth safe while finding a way to aid the outer planets and maintain commerce. But there was also the other troubling obvious problem of tracking down an enemy who had disappeared. As the logistic and convoy systems became dire, we have scheduled support units to move interactively with search teams. We want to coordinate the movement of essential goods and people with an acceptable risk profile."

Whittingham said, "Our orders specifically prioritize the protection of certain mining concerns."

Gallant knew whose mining concerns those were, but he didn't say it out loud. "Those orders include protecting all commerce from enemy raiding."

"They permit asymmetric warfare operation in the furtherance of intelligence collection," added Whittingham.

Gallant said, "By stopping commercial raiding

attacks, we will test the enemy's response and ability to adapt. We will force them to move units to expose their tactical operations."

Gallant observed the officer's reactions. He said, "As you recall, we played the raider game in the Gliese system on the *Warrior* a few years ago. Now the shoe is on the other foot. The raiders seek not only real military value but psychological effects. Its threat to destroy commercial traffic requires us to search for them. So, we must send out hunter-killer groups."

"What do you expect the Titans to do?"

He said, "The Titan command will probably initiate events. We don't know yet how many raiders there are. We will send out reconnaissance scouts and deploy additional sensor arrays."

"All of that will increase the pressure on the Titans," said Whittingham.

He moved closer and spoke softly, "But it will also increase the risk of spreading ourselves too thin."

"But surely we need to stop the Titan fleet from attacking the outer planets as well. That is our primary mission description," Captain Jackson countered.

Gallant said, "War is a lot like poker. It's all about waiting for the right time to go all in."

CHAPTER 16

Nowhere

In the middle of the midwatch, Gallant sat in his command chair watching endless kilometers of space parade past the viewscreen.

His soul was troubled by his disagreement with Alaina. It was a burden from which he knew no escape. He considered retiring to his cabin and listening to music. Music released him from all things sad. It was no coincidence that he found music in harmony with nature.

As he let his mind play one of his favorite songs, thoughts materialized from nowhere. One moment his mind was empty and then . . .

I'd met her on my first day on Elysium. I'm certain of that. Sometime during dinner. The encounter was different from normal introductions people usually experience, though. It was at a serious government gathering that she interrupted with panache. She was dressed in rugged outdoor hiking gear, and she marched boldly into the room, a portrait of a rebellious soul. She was a young vibrant woman with a hunger for adventure. Hers was a hypnotic beauty. After seeing her, I stopped paying attention to anything else.

There were lots of influential people there. They had greeted me warmly, and I thought I was important too. I had been invited to discuss vital geopolitical and genetic issues, but suddenly those concerns seemed less critical after she arrived. I was immensely impressed after being introduced to her. I said I was glad to make her acquaintance. She was thorny and sparky and friendly, all at once. And though it seems unlikely, I can't remember a single thing she said. Throughout the evening, I just stared at her face as she spoke. A remarkable relationship was forming.

Other people jostled for my attention because there were essential matters that needed to be resolved, but when she asked, "can we talk?" and left me a note with her address, I said, 'Yes.' I hoped she was interested in me, but I thought I might be projecting my own wishes on to her.

She left me there, and I soon felt an ache from missing her. Something was different. I was in a new world, and everything that happened after that moment was intertwined with duty versus emotions, a turmoil of uneasy memories. When we met the next day, she told me that she had strong feelings and bold ideas for her people and our situation. But our time was misspent. She said she had a political agenda, but I wondered if it was personal to me. It was not a promising start. Though I had achieved something toward getting close to my heart's desire, I was sad and unsettled. What was wrong?

Later, we embarked on a journey to the Brobdingnag Mountain, and during that experience, I fell in love with her. Being alone hadn't been a heartache before I met her, but now it was. I wished I could have my heart's desire, but I was already bound by military duties. And you don't get your wishes there. However, during our quest, I was surprised at her indifference to being naked. And when she placed a finger on top of the scar on my left shoulder and traced the scar down my back, it was as if her touch had magic powers. It was the first time we made love.

Another adventure soon followed. It led to being attacked by a dragor that materialized out of the shadows. With one scrabble of claws, the dragor was up behind me and then quickly turned and came again. She shot the beast and saved my life that night.

I couldn't stop thinking about her. It overshadowed my days and nights. I was hopelessly in love without the means to defend myself from all its implications. I had never been good with affairs, and the only other meaningful one in my life had ended badly. So, I didn't have good coping skills. I couldn't adequately explain my professional life to her, and it led to complications. The pessimist in me thought there was no chance for the two of us.

Military and political events overtook us and drove us together into a maze of events that both brought us closer while simultaneously wedging us apart through distance. Together, we confronted and fought dangers.

She was sexy, attractive, and right for me. But I was as reluctant to commit to a relationship as ever. I failed to make my feelings clear to her.

To my ineffable joy, things eventually fell into place, and we married. That makes me luckier than most, and I am happier now because of her.

She is often asked, "How do you cope with your husband being away so often?"

She replies, "Well, all things considered, it is a wonderful arrangement even if he's gone repeatedly. It's not for everyone, but it is for us. Every time he comes home, it's like meeting for the first time. We hold hands like teenagers and cherish our days together."

I'm satisfied with that answer.

The ship's bell rang, signaling the end of the watch, and the end of Gallant's daydream.

However, the daydream had triggered ideas about his life and heritage that had been percolating in his subconscious. He considered how genetic engineering played a significant role in his experiences.

It occurred to him that decrypting the enemy's communication and translating it into human speech required using the unique species characteristics. The Titan's genetic engineering and Chameleon's AI chip implants might play a vital role. He decided to send a message to Bletchley Park that summarized his insights.

CHAPTER 17

The Right Stuff

The *Cheshire* stood alone at the edge of the asteroid field astride the traffic lanes between the outer planets and Earth. Captain Charles Jaeger longed to scrutinize the ships that traveled to the nearest port but feared to leave his watch post. He had to pay attention to surveilling the enemy as well as keeping a protective eye on the vulnerable.

There were hundreds of transport ships, thousands of cargo ships, all conscientiously crossing an ocean of space, leaving one port weighted down with people and goods, all of which possessed intrinsic value, to travel to a destination of even greater importance, where an adventitious transaction would occur despite the inherent dangers of war. Their courage to persevere means the United Planets war machine endures.

At the first sign of trouble, a call would go out from the commercial ship with the expectation that a rescuing warship would save them. Unfortunately, that was not always the case.

Stealthily sneaking from corner to corner, the *Cheshire* noted several unremarkable ships in transit. She watched the blizzard of commerce journey throughout the solar system, though she could offer reassurance to but a few.

Jaeger was lucky to have command of the *Cheshire*. Sitting in his command chair, he couldn't imagine a better assignment. He ordered his sensor operators to make a maximum effort. He wanted reports on the comings and goings of everything nearby. The problem was, he hated waiting. He looked over his command console and examined the engine readings. Normal. There was nothing else to occupy his attention. He waited for a sighting of a Titan ship. Yesterday, they had located one, but it was now far behind them. It was simultaneously frustrating and boring. There were any number of other activities he would have preferred to be doing but waiting was all he could manage. The limits of the sensor array were significant, even on this advanced ship.

Compared to the enormity of space, his tiny vessel was its own world, inhabited by a strange mixture of characters. One such character was a young midshipman who incessantly peppered Jaeger with naive questions at every opportunity.

The midshipman of the watch, Midshipman Barry Green, asked Jaeger, "Have you killed a lot of the enemy, sir?"

"Yes. I have."

"Does it ever get to you?"

"It does," replied Jaeger.

Surprisingly, the young man revealed, "I'm not sure I'm cut out for all this."

Nodding knowingly, Jaeger acknowledged, "I've had my own doubts over the years."

"Really, sir?"

"It's true."

"Gee. I had no idea that even you might . . . I mean . . . I thought it would all be different."

"So did I."

"Maybe I'm just wrong for this job," said the midshipman.

"It's natural to wonder about the right and wrong of our choices. You're a young man. You'll figure it out."

"When?"

"It takes its own time, but it does happen."

The OOD interrupted. "Contacts, sir. IFF shows they are a known friendly. There are six transports from the Jupiter moons on course to a rendezvous point where they plan to meet escorts ships."

"Very well. We'll keep a watchful eye on them until they reach safety."

Over the next few hours, Jaeger kept contact with a convoy of six transports carrying women and children from the outer bases. The time passed quietly. It reminded him of the peace and calm of the woods behind his home in Missouri. But at the end of the watch, he went to his cabin to rest.

After a while, he stretched out and waited for

time to pass. He hoped sleep would find him. He lay flat, then on his side and then flat again. He couldn't reject the thoughts troubling him. He considered his responsibilities and his crew's safety. It was better to lie there than show his anxious face around the ship. He was never good at wearing a false smile though he did enjoy chatting with the crew.

For a few more breaths he lay on his cot, then he gave up and returned to the bridge.

Jaeger examined the readouts of the nearby asteroid field. Nothing concerning jumped out at him. One large rock and a few smaller ones were clustered to port. He scanned the other directions, but again there was nothing concerning. In this uncharted region, he was dangerously close.

"CIC, do you have detailed scans of the area?"

"Not yet, Captain. We need a few more minutes."

"What about long-range scans?"

"Not yet, sir."

A few minutes later, the OOD reported, "New contact, sir. Enemy vessels. Two."

Jaeger fidgeted in his chair.

The OOD reported, "Contacts are two Titan destroyers, sir. On an intercept course with the six transports which are still several hours from their escorts."

"Space just became an unwelcoming place," said Jaeger. "OOD sound battle stations."

AGUA! AGUA!

Sounded the Klaxon. The crew scurried about making their way to their stations.

He ordered the ship to approach the newcomers cautiously. There was no reaction from the destroyers. The *Warrior's* stealth was holding.

"Set an intercept course to the two destroyers."

Jaeger made random erratic course changes on the off chance that he might have been detected. That never actually materialized because of the *Cheshire's* incredible stealth.

The *Cheshire* reached firing position before the enemy reached the convoy.

Jaeger dropped out of stealth mode just long enough to launch four missiles. Then he went into stealth and changed course. The missiles were able to damage one enemy ship. He repeated this exercise several times. He was able to confuse and hurt the enemy sufficiently so that they broke off and left the area.

The six transports went merrily on their way, never aware of how their journey might have ended otherwise.

CHAPTER 18

Full of Promise

Kate Mahoney's life was not as simple as it once had been, and lately she was exhausted, well, not just lately. She felt drained forever. Endless work schedules and demanding deadlines will do that even if they are self-imposed. Her only respite were the few moments every day when she looked at the faded photograph she took from her pocket. When you lose someone, you love, their memory becomes a treasure and Kate was able to find strong motivation from her mother's memory.

Each morning, Kate woke with her mind percolating with creative ideas that had inhabited her dreams. She often skipped breakfast to get to the workroom early. But the site would still be asleep and the power to the computer system would be off. She had to crawl under her desk to switch on the electrical panel. Then, she sat waiting for a few minutes while the system booted up.

When he arrived, Logan muttered, "You're here already?"

"I am," she said grumpily. She didn't mention that she arrived uncomfortably early because she was fanatically afraid to be late.

Logan gulped down a cup of thick black coffee to get himself energized for his day. Then he sat, spine erect, feet planted firmly on the deck, inspecting the computer monitor and all its many mysterious aspects.

She pulled the cover off the computer. It was extremely complicated with more buttons, switches, and keys than her previous version. Someone had upgraded the device. That pleased her.

There were manuals on a nearby shelf which she barely noticed. She wouldn't need them.

She said, "I have the latest communication intercepts."

Logan said, "Why bother feeding that into the computer? It won't help. It can crunch on them just as easily as all the others and with no more success. Admit it, we're stumped."

She sighed. "We can't be bound by Plato's cave of ignorance."

"Why do you do that?"

"Do what?"

"Mix a stew of metaphors into a cocktail of irrelevant ideas?"

She laughed out loud. "You're complaining about *my* mixed metaphors?"

"You know what I mean," said the exasperated

ensign. "I've enough ancient Egyptian issues to think about without you throwing in ancient Greeks as well."

"What I'm getting at is the way we are thinking about this problem. Perhaps we are making too broad an interpretation of the multi-lingual combination."

Logan grunted. "Do you mean that we are over-complicating the translation?"

Kate said, "Right. Let's revisit the Rosetta Stone analogy. In the 19th century, Napoleon Bonaparte's army engineers discovered a stone slab in 1799 near the town of Rosetta after they invaded Egypt. In 1801, British defeated the French and acquired the artifact."

Logan nodded. "I know all that."

Undeterred, Kate continued, "The stone featured a decree issued in 196 BC by Egypt's ruler, Ptolemy V, testifying to his generosity and devoutness. The decree was written on the stone in three ways: first, the top text was in the hieroglyphics used by priests; second, the middle text was in the ancient Egyptian Demotic script used by commoners; and finally, the bottom text was in ancient Greek. The use of hieroglyphics died out after the fourth century, and the writing system became an enigma to scholars. The discovery of the Rosetta Stone helped academics to crack the ancient Egyptian code of hieroglyphics."

Logan said, "Just as the Rosetta Stone translates across three very different languages, we need to translate across the Titan–Chameleon–Human languages. But I don't see an ancient text lying around that will help us."

"Don't be so negative," said Kate petulantly. "I propose using common language patterns from each language as a basis for developing an AI self-learning algorithm that will create its own translator."

"Good luck with that."

She gave him a caustic look with furrowed brows. "Everyone likes their secrets. The Titan's constructed this code. One thing that I've found is that the Titan databases were distorted by their prejudices and historic experiences. The Chameleon have their biases too. We can exploit these known biases to find patterns."

"The encryption is layered, and we should try to decode it a layer at a time. The first step is to separate and extract the layers. The first layer should be based upon the biology of the aliens. Next, we can try to layer on my algorithm."

Kate adjusted the network connection and interface. She transcribed the results. Then, she set about to make inexplicable changes to her program. After the day's work, she had no place to be and little desire to return to her sleeping cubical. The tiny cubical was just a stall with a cot, sink, and shower, hardly the most desirable of accommodations, but space was at a premium in the excavated bunker. She assumed that Logan was so attuned to military life that such inconveniences went unnoticed. So, she worked late into the night.

The next day, she found the translation results disappointing.

"Your decryption is gibberish," said Logan.

"Maybe my algorithm is wrong," said Kate in disgust.

Seeing her troubled expression, he asked, "What are you afraid of?"

She thought for a moment. She was afraid of failing in her lofty purpose, but she wouldn't reveal that. She had to keep that hidden by burying it as if it was submerged in a frozen river. After a minute, she muttered, "Come. We have to keep working."

They had sent progress reports to Gallant for over a month, but they were surprised when a response arrived.

"Kate! Kate! Great news," exclaimed Logan throwing open the lab door.

She turned to greet him. Her face lit up expectantly. "That's wonderful. Wait, don't tell me! Don't tell me! Let me guess."

Placing her hands on either side of her head, she contorted her face into a prune and said, "Humm!"

Then she burst out, "You've found a symmetry pattern?"

"No," said Logan with a smirk.

Kate gave him the evil eye and tried again. "Huh! You've found a probabilistic correlation?"

"No. I have . . ." started Logan, but she broke in again.

"No! No! Don't tell me." She closed her eyes for a full minute and then said, "You've produced a self-programming nanobot that decrypts?"

Exasperated, Logan grabbed her by the shoulders and said, "No. Will you listen for a minute? This is important."

"Okay. What?"

"I've received a message from Admiral Gallant. He sent some suggestions for us to consider."

"What's his idea?"

"He thinks that since the Chameleon have AI chips embedded in their brainstem, we should include an element of their biology in our algorithm."

"How can we do that?"

"He sent an encephalograph of a typical Chameleon brain for us to use as a basis."

"Wow! I would never have thought of that. Where did he get that?"

"From the deep secret files of SIA, I imagine. It doesn't matter. We got it now."

She said, "Gallant's idea could be a breakthrough. I've been so buried in the details that I didn't recognize it. He may have unlocked the door. I think we can now go through it and solve this mystery."

"Let's get started on that."

Gallant's suggestion, written in scientific jargon, espoused integrating genetic engineering traits with communication protocols, so much so that Kate began to suspect it was his obsession. But she couldn't pretend that it was without merit. Though she might have been trying to sooth her bruised ego for needing help.

Kate and Logan kept working all that day and the next.

Finally, Kate said, "I have a new algorithm."

"How?" asked Logan.

"My curiosity led to an epiphany."

Logan stared at her.

"When I say, 'epiphany,' I mean, I stole the basic form from Gallant's idea, and I came to realize the missing final key while examining it."

After analyzing her work, Logan said, "I think we've found our own Rosetta Stone. This new algorithm just might translate across the Titan-Chameleon-Human languages."

"Let's run a series of simulations using it on the latest Titan military communication traffic," said Kate. "We can collect the data and send the translated communications to the *Constellation*."

"I agree," said Logan. "This algorithm is full of promise."

CHAPTER 19

The Noose Tightens

Despite the heroics of his recon ships, Gallant got conflicting sightings and confusing information. The intelligence showed that the Titans are consolidating their forces. They are moving lots of resources. But their targets were uncertain.

Gallant prepared to meet the challenge. The staff meeting in the admiral's war room had become routine and tough questions were often addressed.

"What would Machiavelli do?" asked Whittingham.

Gallant snorted. "The Titans aren't that similar to human behavior."

"Yes, sir, but they are brilliant, rigid, and manipulative. I believe that very much mimics the behavior of a human sociopath."

"But Niccolò Machiavelli? The purveyor of 'The ends justify the means.'"

Whittingham said, "He wrote *The Prince*, which

described how to seize and hold power. It considered whether to exterminate a resisting population. It was brutal, bloody, and cynical."

"I have read his treatise. Personally, I prefer the inspiring and uplifting ideas of Rousseau."

"Of course, sir. But Machiavelli had a low opinion of people. He believed major social change could only be achieved through violence because the existing stakeholders would resist with all their might. He approved of lying and murder. If you look at human history, a lot of his methods have been employed. He was cunning at figuring out what obstacles stood in his way and how to obliterate them. The Titans are more accomplished at these traits. They are murderous, cold-heart tyrants."

Gallant said, "In the five hundred years since he wrote *The Prince*, we've made a lot of technological progress."

"That's true, but we are still beset by jealousy, power-mongering, treachery, and aggression. Those are characteristics that are manifest in the Titans even more so than humans."

Gallant scowled. "I must admit, that is not an unreasonable comparison. The recent enemy movements show that Admiral Vvorn is putting a complex plan into effect. But he has masked his movements so well that we are unable to keep track of where his major units are or where they are likely to strike first."

"Though the Titans have successfully concealed their disposition, we know their ultimate intention is the extermination of humanity. This must mean that Earth will be targeted in some nefarious way. If we can guess the enemy's plan, we may be able to parry his thrust. So, I ask again, sir, 'what would Machiavelli do?'"

CHAPTER 20

Without Dissent

The Commander-in-Chief of the Titan Battle Fleet stood on the bridge of the spacecraft carrier *Vespa* basking in the glory of his victories. With powerful shoulders and a razor-sharp mind, Admiral Vvorn was known for his innovative talents, which marked him unique amongst Titans. He was poised on the balls of his feet as if ready to leap into action and make his new masterpiece plan a triumph.

The *Vespa* was the newest carrier class and flagship of the fleet. Her pilots were trained to perfection. Her starfighters were all upgraded. But the fleet's six carriers had been reduced to four after Vvorn sent a pair back home. However, besides them were six monster dreadnaughts and six battlecruisers, as well as many escorts.

Planning for the upcoming operation had Vvorn grinding away. His staff was tactically excellent, and his fleet was in high spirits. His chief-of-staff, Captain Kkag, had a reputation as a bulldog. According to several war game simulations, he hoped there might be a misdirection play that could fool the humans.

"The time is ripe," said Vvorn. "If we delay any longer, the enemy will grow in strength. Soon more of the United Planets forces will return to the solar system, and they will be looking to evict us."

"That is true, Admiral. The problem is that they are moving their forces around, and we've lost sight of several major elements. These could pop up unexpectedly and cause problems."

"That is even more reason to move now and put pressure on them to fear our deployment. Let *them* wonder about our intentions. Let *them* guess where to place their forces."

Each day, Vvorn's blunt manner set the standard for clear, precise communication. He encouraged his subordinates to speak frankly and develop an optimal strategy. He began to outline some possible war orders to coordinate the different elements of the campaign. The vectors of ships were calculated to precise points. He assigned priority targets himself. Full-scale planning was underway because time wasn't on his side.

Vvorn said, "Our goal is to destroy or permanently cripple the human military so that we can consolidate our conquest of the outer planets. The basic plan should start with a decoy. Then a major assault on Earth would be unleashed with a bombardment by our dreadnaughts simultaneously with a starfighter attack from our carriers. An infantry assault on the Earth would complete their destruction. These four naval units must be closely coordinated."

Because of his love of probabilities, Kkag had ran countless simulations considering every possibility. He said, "Each battle plan option has its advantages and disadvantages."

Vvorn said, "I've seen your report. I what to know our best chance for total victory."

"My simulations show that option I has a 93% chance of total success with less than a 1% chance of a setback. Option II has a 95% chance of total success but with a 3% chance of a setback."

"What do you consider to be setback?"

"I can't guarantee that there is a zero percent chance of defeat. But I have found that there is only a small potential for the human defenses to hold us off and less than one percent chance for our fleet to suffer a significant loss. In other words, even if we fail to eradicate all human life, we will inflict great harm to the Earth without suffering significant losses to our fleet."

"Good. The key to our endeavor will be concealing our intentions for as long as possible. This will create the element of surprise and breed uncertainty in the enemy."

Kkag said, "By moving our fleet units in fits and starts, we can make it nearly impossible for any enemy surveillance to keep tabs on our ships or to determine our rendezvous points. Our plans will be completely obscured."

Vvorn said, "Good. Good. That is what I want, to keep them off-balance and guessing for as long as possible.

"Then the destruction of Earth is assured!" concluded Kkag.

Vvorn looked at Kkag and then at the other members of the planning staff. They all looked very much alike. In fact, he wondered at the uniformity of their advice. They all agreed on a plan to attack, attack, attack. Everyone embraced that single concept. There wasn't a single dissenting voice. No alternative strategy was offered.

Was there no other path to victory?

In the back of his mind, that troubled him, though he couldn't put his finger on exactly why.

Big Brother.

The thought startled him.

Where have I heard that name before?

It came to him as an unsettling memory. The name was from a human book he had examined in his studies of his enemy. Somehow this book popped into his mind while he was looking at his obedient staff officers.

How could that be relevant?

CHAPTER 21

Faded Photograph

Major James Steward saw the Titan invasion force approaching the Bletchley Park asteroid. He assessed the enemy's strength. His company of Marines wasn't going to be enough.

His distress call was sent in the clear. "To all ships: URGENT! Base 83 is under Titan assault. Request immediate assistance. Repeat, URGENT! Base 83 is under Titan assault. Request immediate assistance."

Kate was startled when she heard the first alarm bells ringing. She knew that danger was imminent, but she had infinite faith in James Steward. He wouldn't let her down. She went on finishing her work and transferring as much as she could onto a backup flash drive.

Logan burst into her lab and shouted, "Hey! Get a move on. We've to go to the safe room until this is over."

"Is that really necessary? There's still so much more to do."

"Kate, that vault has thick titanium walls designed to protect us for just this kind of emergency. Let's get there and wait this out. I'm sure Major Steward knows what he's doing."

"Okay. Let me download this last decryption run. It's promising. I think we may have the code-breaking solution. I don't want to lose it. We have to get it to Admiral Gallant."

Kate lingered for another few minutes but finally made her way to the safe room. She entered the shelter in the center of the bastion just as the jolt from the first missile hit the asteroid. Logan was right behind her and sealed the hatch shut.

They felt the missile bombardment and subsequent gun battle outside the protected room.

Kate and Logan hunkered down and hoped help would arrive in time.

Steward was under no illusion about help arriving in time. He did not want anyone to guess at his trepidation. Lack of sleep and worry coupled with a sense of guilt worked to shorten his temper. He knew that this was bad.

It was all too soon before more Titan missiles

struck with brutal power. Several destroyers stood off and fired missiles and plasma weapons. They demolished Steward's only two defensive missile batteries.

A Titan assault craft hovered into position.

The marines were stationed in key mountain positions on the asteroid to give them the best firing lanes. They sent a hail of bullets and lasers upward. It wasn't enough. The outer defenses were quickly breached by the Titan forces.

The battle was now on the asteroid surface and in the trenches surrounding the Bletchley Park bunker. The marines stood behind a barricade at the site's entrance portal.

Straight down the access portholes one thousand meters, led to a series of connected tunnels two meters in diameter. The walls of the chamber were airtight and connected to chambers that quartered the marines. One large chamber contained the communication and computer equipment. There were other smaller chambers required to maintain the atmosphere within the site.

Steward stationed guards at key access hatches. Guns flashed, but so far, only a trickle of Titans had penetrated the marines' position.

At that, they rallied and nearly threw back the first wave of attackers. Steward ran into the thick of battle to help restore the situation.

"Here they come again," cried one marine. A few men fired to hold the barricade.

The main body of the defenders continued a ragged fire of light weapons.

The Titans remained undercover and didn't move forward for several minutes.

Steward said, "They're not fools to waste ammunition without a purpose. They're up to something. Send a detail to cover our flank."

"All together now," Steward bellowed. "Forward!"

They fired from the barricade with renewed vigor.

But soon, the Titans broke through the last line of defense. The remaining defenders were killed. The portal was exposed to the enemy.

What's happening?

He found himself separated from his men.

Regaining his bearings, he continued to shoot at the blinding flashes coming his way.

He blinked and realized that he was surrounded!

BANG!

Am I hit?

Piercing pain in his shoulder told him where the bullet had grazed him. He dropped to the ground. Perhaps, it would be a worthwhile death. His fighting madness ebbed away, replaced by a wave of grief.

He got up and reproached himself, "Get going."

Someone grabbed his arm. "This way, Major."

Steward felt the heavy responsibility weigh him down.

It isn't fair.

Steward and a marine team gathered at the entrance to the underground tunnel.

"Stay there and wait for my signal," he said to his men.

Yet, he couldn't ignore the fact that retreating would seal them into the bunker without the means to hold it.

He ordered, "Follow me."

The smoke and damage from the bombardment hid Steward as he crawled into the subterranean tunnel. The marines flooded into the tunnel and entered the deep Bletchley Park bunker. Once his men were inside the tunnels, he stepped through the security hatch and into the compartment. He climbed down the portal entry ladder.

The dust and debris of broken ramparts and bulkheads were everywhere. The bunker was in a state of devastation and confusion, but the tunnels were still airtight.

The stench of stale air hit Steward as he entered the tunnel. He realized that the ventilation system might be damaged.

Steward ordered, "Covering fire!"

Dat-dat-dat-dat-dat-dat-dat-dat-dat-dat!

A sergeant asked, "How long can we hold out?"

Steward chided him. "Until help arrives. Look sharp. Move the men forward."

As the Titans penetrated deeper, the marines resisted at every juncture.

The heavy fighting continued. The human wreckage of the wounded, dying, and dead littered the area.

Thpff! Thpff! Thpff!

An explosion nearly knocked Steward flat. His senses felt all wrong. For several minutes he shook off the effects of the concussion. The acrid fumes of fire stung his nose as he lay on the ground. It was several minutes before he was able to struggle to his feet. His skull felt as if it were split in two. Blood trickled down his left ear. He tried to dismiss the pain.

Steward and several marines stood guard at their entrance to the main bunker tunnel.

Steward said, "Sergeant, secure the entry hatches into this tunnel."

"Will do."

But before the marines moved, a whisper formed in Steward's mind . . .

There's little time.

Then as if on cue, several Titans emerged from an entry hatch thirty meters to Steward's right, their weapons raised and pointing at Steward and his men.

No one moved. They waited a full second in frozen silence.

Then, more Titans emerged from a hatch to Steward's left. They were out of breath and surprised at the gathering before them.

Everyone was frozen as if the surprise each group felt had left them all in suspended animation. The shock caused everyone to swing their guns back and forth, uncertain where to aim and who to fire at.

Steward couldn't tell who fired first, but nearly simultaneously, a score of automatic handguns and lasers were set ablaze. An intense crossfire at close range ensued.

Pfft! pfft! pfft!
Thpff! Thpff! Thpff!
Over a hundred bullets flew around within ten seconds.
Splat! Splat!
The laser blasts lit up the compartment.

A strange lull descended after a minute as soldiers fell to the ground screaming and clutching bloody holes in their bodies. The survivors were forced into individual firefights.

It was another minute as the fighters began ejecting their empty magazines from their weapons, and their hands smacked over their bodies in search of another clip. As clips were rammed home, the remaining men began looking at who was a threat to them.

Steward was kneeling on one knee. His battle-armor had stopped most of the laser blasts and some of the heavy caliber bullets, but not all. His left arm was bleeding from a bullet hole. The mingling of burning flesh from laser wounds and the stench of gunpowder sickened his stomach and seared the back of his throat.

He heard the crack of his sergeant's skull before the splattering blood reached him. The sergeant collapsed to the ground.

Many Titans were on the ground, dozens of bullet holes leaking their life's blood into a gigantic pool of red ooze.

Pling! pling! pling!
Thpff! Thpff! Thpff!
Once more, the staccato drum of gunfire went

off as the automatic handguns released another hail of destruction. This time the accuracy was even worse than before. The painful wounds and blurry eyes made aiming impossible.

Steward felt a bullet hit him. It was like being kicked in the chest. His breath seemed to ooze away as the bullet struck hard. Everything was spinning. There was a roar in his ears. He dropped to the ground listening to the thumping of his heart.

There was only one Titan still standing. The Titan's shot missed wildly.

Dizzy and hurting, Steward fired.

Pling! pling!

Did I hit him?

The Titan fired again.

Thpff!

Another lull followed.

Several Titans lying on the ground were still firing wildly, hitting nothing.

Thpff! Thpff!

The last living Titan's gun sounded out a series of clicks. It was empty.

Steward's gun was also empty, and he had no more magazine clips. He threw the gun to the ground and looked for a weapon.

The Titan reloaded first and fired.

Thpff!

The bullet penetrated Steward's battle-armor and entered his abdomen. It felt as if he had been kicked. He lurched and groaned, then rolled on the ground clutching his side listening to the frantic pounding of his heart. He couldn't catch his breath. Everything was spinning. He tried to keep his eyes open, but the cavern became a blur.

He sat against the wall as specks of blood extruded from his mouth. He felt the full effect of being physically ill; nauseated, confused, and freezing cold.

He glanced at the sergeant's body sprawled on the ground like a discarded rag doll.

Is he dead?

He saw the last Titan still struggling.

Steward managed to pick up a rifle from a fallen marine.

The Titan's next shot missed wildly, and before he could fire again, Steward fired.

Did I hit him?

Steward listened to dying enemy gurgling for a full minute. Then all motion in the tunnel ceased, and the silence became absolute. He was the only one moving. He crawled closer to the safe room, where he knew Kate and Logan were barricaded.

The searing pain of his abdomen was complimented by a strange coppery taste in his mouth. Fear started to sling snakelike through his belly.

Hell, I need help.

But there was no help.

It's a hard thing, realizing you are about to die. Not next year or next month—but here and now. You start thinking about your life as if it were an abstract object—to be given away as if it didn't make a difference to you personally. But it was personal. The most personal thing possible.

Steward propped himself against the safe room door and leveled his rifle down the tunnel, waiting for more Titans.

I'm going to lie here until I die.

Twelve hours after receiving Major James Steward's distress call, the *Constellation* sent a rescue team to the surface of the asteroid.

The Titans had already done their worst and departed.

When Gallant reached the Bletchley Park bunker, he saw the aftermath of heavy weapon fire and missile detonations. The impact and explosions must have been huge because the damage was devastating. Though some of the tunnels were still airtight there remained an unnerving quiet.

Gallant crashed through the main hatch and made his way through the main tunnel, passing bodies of marines and Titan warriors, the remnants of hand-to-hand combat.

When he reached the center of the inner sanctuary, he found the safe room. Its hatch had been breached by a massive explosion. Major Steward's body was crumpled against the wall.

Gallant pulled back the twisted metal hatch and shone a light into the room.

His eyes fell on the body of Daniel Logan. He was curled in a fetal position in the center of the room, his body riddled with a dozen holes all oozing blood.

I'm too late!

Gallant knelt. He turned Logan's body over and found what Logan had been curled around.

It's Kate!

Her expressionless face looked strangely at peace. But her emerald eyes were as wide as saucers, and her skin was alabaster white. Then Gallant saw what he feared most—a row of crimson flowers blossoming on Kate's chest.

There are many shades of personal grief, and in that poignant moment, Gallant experienced them all.

An image of Midshipman Michael Gabriel, another young fallen comrade, flashed before him.

Some hurts are too deep to forget.

"No," he cried, shaking his head in helpless frustration. "This shouldn't be."

He removed his helmet to wipe his eyes as they welled up.

Leaning down, he touched his lips to Kate's temple and whispered, "So young. So full of promise."

In his sorrow, he remained over her for what seemed a long time. Then, he noticed that she gripped something in her hand. He pried open Kate's clenched fist to reveal her two most precious possessions, which she had protected with her last breath of life.

The room remained eerily silent as Henry Gallant rose and left with a flash drive full of decryption secrets.

Kate Mahoney remained, her hand still clutching a faded photograph.

CHAPTER 22

War Paint

Gallant sat across from Collingsworth in the admiral's stateroom. The two men wore equally grim faces. Collingsworth had taken the *Yorktown* as his flagship. It remained in orbit around Earth with the new Home Fleet, as a staunch safeguard.

Gallant said, "Though Vvorn was successful in destroying the Home Fleet, he suffered losses and damage that he had to recover from. Over the last few months, he has replenished and refitted his ships, and he is now ready to challenge Earth's defenses. He wants to launch a massive bombardment and overwhelm all our battle stations, starfighters, and ships."

"But we've been reenforced and strengthened as well."

"Yes, but we started with the wreckage of the Home Fleet. It wasn't possible to do as much as the Titans."

Gallant was anxious to discuss the decryption of recent Titan communications, but the sting of losing Kate Mahoney and Daniel Logan was still fresh in his mind. He flinched as the image of Kate's body flashed into his mind.

He took a deep breath and paused for a moment before he said, "Using Bletchley Park's algorithm, we have decoded the latest Titan operations communication."

Collingsworth waited eagerly.

"We have concluded that the Titans will send a decoy force to attack Mars. It will include a cruiser destroyer squadron with some transports. They hope to draw off some ten to twenty percent of Earth's defenders. Then four dreadnaughts, six battlecruisers, and cruiser destroyer squadrons will bombard Earth. Far behind the carriers with two dreadnaughts will provide starfighter cover. In addition, transport assault convoy will trail behind."

"If we let this attack proceed as planned, we're in trouble," said Collingsworth with furrows forming on his brow.

"Very much so."

Collinsworth asked, "What is your assessment of Earth's survival chances if we keep all our forces to defend Earth and face this attack head-on?"

Gallant grimaced. "If we let him proceed with his plan as it is designed, our chances are poor. Mars will certainly face devastating damage. Earth's chances of survival would be," Gallant shrugged, "dark."

Collingsworth let a small groan slip from his lips.

"Vvorn has the power and the numbers on his side," said Gallant. "He will send his dreadnaughts in to bombard Earth's defenses with the first wave of starfighters. We could expect a fate like that of the Home Fleet. We might be able to survive for a while, but subsequent waves of starfighters will wither our defenses. Then their heavy ships will launch missile after missile until all is obliterated."

"So, you are convinced that we can't win in a straight-up slugging match?" asked Collingsworth.

"That will only lead to failure."

"Can you offer another option?"

"Yes, but it is very risky."

"We're in the risk-taking business, young man," said the older sailor. "Please continue."

Gallant laid out his plan while Collingsworth's frown deepened with each additional detail.

"You want to divide our forces?" asked an astonished Collingsworth.

"Yes."

"But that's exactly what Vvorn wants."

"No, sir. He wants us to send our squadrons after a decoy, taking them away from the main battle. What I want to do is use two small squadrons to stab Vvorn, where he is most vulnerable. He will then have to make some unpalatable redeployment choices. The Titan plan will be completely disrupted, giving us an opportunity to defeat him in detail."

"You weren't kidding when you said this plan

was risky."

"If my plan works, it will significantly improve Earth's survival chances."

"And if it fails?" asked Collingsworth.

With a stone-cold face, Gallant said, "Then Earth will face certain doom."

"Then, you had better put on your war paint," said Collinsworth. "And one more thing, Henry."

"Yes, sir?"

"Don't fail!"

CHAPTER 23

Gambit

Captain John Roberts boarded the battlecruiser *Indefatigable* and reported to Captain Donahue, a middle-aged man with a dour, rather melancholy face. Roberts wondered if the man were merely unfortunate in his appearance or if he were perpetually unhappy.

"Glad to have you on board, Roberts," said Donahue without a glimmer of enthusiasm.

"Thank you," said Roberts extending his hand.

Donahue nodded at the gesture. He sat behind his stateroom desk with a pile of documents and maps strewn before him. He said, "I'm going to need your best judgment to keep me apprised of the enemy's movements at all times."

"Of course. That's my job. The *Warrior* will get close to convoy Alpha and detail its position, course, and speed. I will make a particular effort to get the direction vectors for the covering force. Admiral Gallant has given me intelligence on the enemy's strength and intentions."

Donahue said, "We will begin our attack once they emerge from the edge of the asteroid field. The field will afford us radar cover until the last possible moment, thus ensuring surprise."

Roberts respected the plan of attack. After all, given the limited units that Gallant gave his squadron, there was only so much he could do. However, Roberts expected that surprise and speed would play a major role in panicking the vulnerable assault convoy.

"The *Warrior* will be ready," reassured Roberts.

Donahue planned to split his squadron into a battlecruiser and two cruisers to face off against the Titan cruiser destroyer covering force, while his remaining four destroyers would ravage the thin-skinned transports. They didn't have to destroy them all, just frighten them enough to cause Vvorn to alter his plans and send some relief ships.

That was Donahue's hope. It remained to be seen if he could pull this off.

Though Roberts didn't consider Donahue as solid as Gallant, he could be relied upon to execute this assignment. He would herd his squadron into an intercepting attack position and press home his advantage.

As the meeting ended, Roberts was certain that Donahue's face was even more despondent than when he first came in.

When Roberts returned to the bridge of the *Warrior*, it felt warm and hospitable. The bridge crew exchanged welcoming glances. He was confident there would be no hesitation in their performance.

The OOD reported, "We have a solid fix on convoy Alpha, sir."

Roberts ordered, "Relay the position to Captain Donahue."

A minute later, the response came.

"Good. Good. Keep us updated," replied Donahue.

The *Warrior* used the Bletchley Park decrypted information to identify and track the Titan assault convoy. It had 100 transports and supply vessels with a covering force of four cruisers and twenty destroyers. Its course vector was a dagger toward Earth. Their cargoes were composed of thousands of troops for the invasion of Earth. The convoy maintained a disciplined course in columns unconcerned about any threats.

Donahue's squadron consisted of 61,000-ton battlecruiser *Indefatigable*, cruisers *Newport* and *Retribution*, and destroyers *Firebrand, Ajax, Hermes,* and *Achilles.* They weaved through the last of the asteroid field on their way toward the enemy convoy.

The *Warrior* acted as their eyes, feeding them a continuous stream of data. This allowed Donahue to maneuver his squadron into position while avoiding the Titan covering force. They plodded carefully behind the enemy remaining out of sight. They only had to wait for Gallant's order to attack.

While the *Warrior* and *Indefatigable* waited, Gallant tensed in his command chair aboard the *Constellation*. His small squadron of ten ships was poised to spring his trap against Vvorn's fleet.

At 0601, the OOD reported, "Message from the *Warrior*, sir."

Gallant read:

> From: *Warrior*
> To: *Constellation*
> The *Warrior* and the *Indefatigable* are in position to engage convoy Alpha.
> *Captain John Roberts*

Gallant fidgeted in his chair and waited some more. Soon another message arrived.

At 0730, the OOD reported, "Message from the *Cheshire*, sir."

Gallant read:

> From: *Cheshire*
> To: *Constellation*
> Enemy fleet is at expected location.
> Formation is as expected.
> Carriers are launching space wing
> Tracking acceleration vectors.
> Initial heading is toward Earth.
> *Captain Charles Jaeger*

He reread the message and thought,
So far, so good
Each passing second seemed longer than the

last one. Gallant licked his lips impatiently.

At 0855, the OOD reported, "Message from the *Yorktown*, sir."

Gallant read:

> From: *Yorktown*
> To: *Constellation*
>> Mars is under bombardment by a cruiser destroyer squadron.
>> Enemy space wing is approaching Earth.
> *Admiral George Collingsworth*

All was in readiness to spring his gambit.

Gallant said, "Good. Good."

At 0900, he ordered a message to be sent.

> From: *Constellation*
> To: *Warrior* and *Indefatigable*
>> Attack.
>> Repeat.
>> Attack.
> *Admiral Henry Gallant*

Aboard the *Warrior*, the OOD reported, "Message from the *Constellation*, sir."

Roberts read:

> From: *Constellation*
> To: *Warrior* and *Indefatigable*
>> Attack.

> Repeat.
> Attack.
> *Admiral Henry Gallant*

A million kilometers away, aboard the *Indefatigable,* Donahue timed his move perfectly. His force came out of stealth mode and drove at full speed toward the convoy. Donahue used drones and spread his small force out to cast the largest radar blip possible, trying to look bigger than he was.

The *Warrior* shaved close to a large asteroid and closed on the convoy. Roberts stood as close as possible to the forward viewscreen as if he wanted to get ahead of his own ship. As Donahue made his run, the *Warrior* lurched forward to supply them with a continuous stream of data on the enemy ships position and course vectors.

The Titan convoy was in a formation of ten rows with ten ships in each row. The escort of four cruisers and twenty destroyers was about three-light minutes ahead of the convoy. At that distance, it would take the escort ten minutes to turn and reach the convoy.

In those ten minutes, Donahue planned to do a lot of damage to the thin-skinned transports.

He radioed the *Warrior*, "I hope we survive this. Good luck."

Roberts said, "Survival is what you have to do after things go wrong. I hope we've planned better than that. Remember, speed is everything. It's all a matter of timing. We must move quickly, or we'll fail."

The *Indefatigable* led with cruisers *Newport* and *Retribution* following in line behind her. The four destroyers, *Firebrand*, *Ajax*, *Hermes*, and *Achilles* formed a separate line formation. The two columns cut through the convoy like a pincer and fired in every direction. The hulls of the transports were easily penetrated by lasers and railguns, so the ships kept their missiles for later action against the escorts.

The *Warrior* joined the action but remained at the rear of the convoy.

The weapons officer reported, "We're within weapon's range, Captain."

It isn't a good policy to open fire at maximum range. The first salvo, patiently calculated and properly aimed, was too precious an opportunity to use lightly. It needed to be optimized for the best effect. So, Roberts waited until he could select an individual target and ordered the first salvo to fire at optimal range with great precision at the Titan ship.

"Commence firing."

It did significant damage. The enemy ship fell

out of formation and limped out of the battle.

The *Warrior* opened fire on the next foremost ship and scored another hit. The firing became rapid and less accurate, but the enemy suffered. Roberts concentrated railguns and missile fire on the transport.

"Grand shooting! Grand!" boomed the chief-of-the-watch in a booming baritone voice.

Roberts's heart beat rapidly as he realized that his efforts had paid off.

The transports were confused at first as to who was firing at them. They soon figured out it didn't matter. What mattered was getting away. There were distress signals from the convoy, and soon escape pods were emitted.

The *Indefatigable*'s larger caliber weapons blew holes through the enemy ships and left them wrecks. Rapidly, one after another many of the transports were eliminated.

When they had done as much damage as possible, the *Indefatigable* and the cruisers turned their attention to the escort screen. While they tangled with the covering force the four UP destroyers continued shelling up the convoy. It was like shooting fish in a barrel.

Alarms sounded throughout the convoy as the Titans fought back.

The *Warrior* and Donahue's four destroyers kept up a steady fire. Switching targets as soon as one of the thin hulled transports showed serious damage. The neat convoy columns scattered into a weird display of radiated escape vectors. Roberts slowed the *Warrior* to avoid passing by the ships. He zig-zagged to get the best firing angles.

They had plenty of time to scan the ships as they approached, and its escort was primed when they reached them. After an hour of heavy bombardment, the convoy protection was weakening.

The convoy escorts finally reached the battle action and opened fire at extreme range. They charged headlong at the *Indefatigable* and splashed radiation on the shields.

Cruisers *Newport* and *Retribution* fired broadsides that knocked out one Titan destroyer. They now had a fair chance in a toe-to-toe slugging match with the remaining Titan ships. However, the enemy was known to be resourceful. As it turned out, they still had a great deal of fight left in them. The ships altered their course to fire their salvos. The Titan ships managed a ragged barrage which wasn't as destructive they had hoped, but nevertheless, damaged the *Retribution.*

As the *Newport* maneuvered to shield the *Retribution,* she exploded in a fiery ball and disappeared.

Donahue ordered the *Indefatigable* to fire as rapidly as possible. He left the *Newport* to cover them while the *Retribution* accelerated toward the enemy.

The engagement remained brutally violent as they closed.

The *Indefatigable* fired salvo after salvo and ripped an enemy cruiser wide open.

The OOD reported, "*Retribution* is a wreck,

barely able to navigate, let alone defend herself."

The enemy destroyers launched missiles at the *Retribution*. She suffered damage, and her captain was forced to abandon ship.

As the battle ebbed and flowed, the enemy ships drew ever closer and more threatening. The ship-to-ship battle was only one hour old, and many had already died.

The *Indefatigable* was engaged but was taking a terrible pounding. To her credit, she was beating up the enemy too.

"Damn them! Damn them all!" came Donahue's baritone voice on the bridge over the din of confusion.

The enemy came on to finish the fight. An update from Roberts swung the *Indefatigable* toward the nearest enemy ship. The ships were now fighting in the clinches.

"Their fire is slackening. I'm sure of it," reported the OOD.

At that critical juncture, Donahue ordered the *Newport* to launch an all-out counterattack by charging at the enemy ships. Despite this tactic, the enemy streamed forward. If anything, the enemy ships continued with renewed ardor. The *Newport's* attack made her the main target of the Titans covering force. After repeated close broadsides, the ship was so severely holed, the crew had to abandon ship.

The engagement between the two forces was hotly contested. The outcome hung by a thread. If it broke against them, all hope would be lost.

With many ships badly damaged, the *Indefat-*

igable was now essentially alone in a desperate battle with the remaining enemy.

The *Indefatigable* was also hit by concentrated fire of the numerous enemy ships and was now a shadow of her former self. The harmony that typified a well-coordinated, finely tuned machine had dissolved. Her engines weren't in their normal rhythm; the ship's motion was slightly erratic. Though Donahue couldn't put a name on the difference, he sensed that the ship and its crew were hurting.

"Mmmm," said Donahue watching the enemy bearing down on him. A wave of apprehension and excitement didn't stop him from calculating his next course of action. He swallowed hard and set his plan of action in motion.

With the enemy cruisers closing on the *Indefatigable*, destroyers *Firebrand, Ajax, Hermes*, and *Achilles* left the transports and closed to support the battlecruiser. They managed to coordinate their fire and throw back the enemy. The weapons' fire from the *Indefatigable* was conducted with so much skill and effect that the enemy finally turned aside.

It was a difficult moment, but Donahue decided to lead his surviving ships away from the convoy.

The Titans were just as eager to escape from the battle, but of the 100 transports, only 44 were still intact, and none were heading toward Earth. They were busy sending out distress messages calling Admiral Vvorn for help.

CHAPTER 24

Queen Sacrifice

Gallant gazed around the bridge of the *Constellation.* Task Force 34 had been reduced to one carrier and a modest cruiser destroyer squadron. It was a small but potent strike force. Gallant hoped it would be enough. It was now poised to strike the second surprise blow against the Titan fleet.

The nine-ship squadron maintained maximum stealth while penetrating the open space between Vvorn's carriers and the Titan convoy Alpha. The squadron was arranged in a single column, the cruisers *Astoria* and *Cassandra* in the lead, followed by the *Constellation,* with the six destroyers last.

When *Warrior* and *Indefatigable* struck the Alpha convoy, Gallant anticipated that Vvorn would deploy some of his fleet to rescue the convoy. Vvorn would then have fewer resources to attack Earth. Gallant hoped this would allow Admiral Collingsworth and the 7th Fleet a respite. This would also give the *Constellation's* starfighters an opportunity to strike the enemy carriers not only from behind but when they were most vulnerable.

However, while knowing your enemy's plan is wonderful, it is by no means enough to stop him. The solution lay in applying fleet tactics effectively. Assumptions don't always turn out to be correct. Your enemy could always pull a surprise of his own.

Gallant waited eagerly for his plan to unfold.

Finally, at 1000: The OOD reported, "Message from the *Warrior*, sir."

Gallant read:

> From: *Warrior*
> To: *Constellation*
> *Warrior* and *Indefatigable* have engaged enemy transport convoy Alpha.
> *Captain John Roberts*

Soon more news reached the *Constellation*.

At 1112, the OOD reported, "Message from the *Cheshire*, sir."

Gallant read:

> From: *Cheshire*
> To: *Constellation*
> The enemy fleet is at the expected location and on the expected course.
> Four carriers are preparing to launch a second wave.
> Two dreadnaughts and escorts sup-

porting.

The initial vector heading is toward Earth.
Captain Charles Jaeger

Gallant felt a great weight pressing down upon him. He had set crucial events into motion, things that could not be undone. Everything depended upon his choices proving correct. The fate of humanity hung in the balance. But Gallant couldn't help the self-doubt that bubbled up. Was he capable of correctly making world-shattering decisions? Could he shoulder the responsibility? Was Neumann correct that only the genetically engineered should be trusted to perform under this circumstance?

Doubt is a killer. It wounds the soul and starves the ego. It leaves uncertainty just when confidence is most needed. He rubbed his brow as if he could wipe the doubt away. But he couldn't simply wish it away. He had to find the will to go forward and hoped the fortitude to continue would rise within him.

Gallant walked into the ready room reviewing the preparations for launching the space wing. As the crew started on flight operations, tension escalated. He had to identify and reconcile conflicting activities. The deck could be a dangerous place with a short runway and little margin for error.

"The enemy carriers are about one light-hour ahead of us," said the OOD, Lieutenant Clay. "Request permission to conduct a long-range scan, sir."

"Granted," said Gallant. "Get a pair of Hawkeyes

up, as well."

"Aye aye, sir."

A few minutes later, Clay ordered, "Launch Hawkeyes."

The Hawkeyes fanned out to cover more of the three-dimensional vacuum before them. Their precision detection gear searching for the enemy.

In the lead, soon Kelsey Mitchel reported, "Enemy fleet sighted. There are four carriers, two dreadnaughts, two battlecruisers, many cruisers, and many destroyers in formation. It's a target-rich environment."

A few minutes later, she reported, "There is a large CSP. I'm playing hide and seek with their sensors,"

Gallant ordered, "Prepare space wing for an all-out attack on the enemy carrier group.

He listened to the buzz around the bridge. They were ready to face the battle.

He spoke over the ship's intercom, "Men and women of the *Constellation*, I am honored to be leading you today. Our mission is to stop the enemy carrier task force from threatening Earth. We will not fail."

Gallant thought, *I trust them.*

At 1323, the OOD reported, "Message from the *Yorktown*, sir."

Gallant read:

> From: *Yorktown*
> To: *Constellation*

> Enemy cruiser destroyer squadron is attacking Mars.
> Enemy space wing is attacking Earth.
> Four dreadnaughts and escorts are attacking Earth.
> *Admiral George Collingsworth*

Gallant looked at the view screen and set his jaw.

The time is now!

He rose from his chair.

At 1324, Gallant ordered, "Launch starfighters!"

The flight crew moved each fighter into position on the catapult. Then raised the blast deflector behind them. Once the flight deck cleared, the hanger depressurized, and the hanger doors slid open to the vacuum of space. The catapult officer initiated the high-speed piston that shot the fighter into space while the pilot throttled the engine. The 90,000-kilo starfighter machine rocketed from 0 to 100 km/s almost immediately.

During normal operations, the crew could launch one fighter every two minutes. During combat, those tolerances were reduced to allow four launches per minute. The pace was both demanding and treacherous.

The starfighters took off in a consecutive series of swooshes.

The UPSS *Constellation* CVS-647 launched its full attack complement at Vvorn's carrier fleet.

Fighters and bombers shot into space and maneuvered into its slot in the attack formation. The space wing formed into an extended eagle formation used for long travel.

The attack wing followed in a diamond pattern. It consisted of Lieutenant Glen Holman's Squadron 6 fighters. Each fighter was eager to engage and wiggled impatiently in their high-g chairs. Lieutenant Lorelei Steward's Squadron 8 bombers were in a staggered layered formation behind them

As group leader, Lieutenant Glen Holman went through flight checks for the squadrons. It was several hours until they reached the enemy. The time passed slowly and tensely.

All too soon, however, they saw their target.

The Titan sensors picked up the starfighters in time to launch their own fighters. The escorts put up a wall of flak and released decoys. The CSP surged forward.

As the space wing approached the Titan carriers, Kelsey Mitchell reported, "Squadron Leaders, I have critical targeting data. Standby for download."

The Titan CSP engaged with Holman's lead fighters.

Holman ordered, "Flight 1 punch a hole through the CSP. Flight 2 fly close bomber support. Flight 3 remains in reserve."

The squadrons went into action and closed on the enemy. The bomber pilots were determined to reach the carriers while the fighters were determined to give them an opening and keep them covered.

"Lock weapons on target," ordered Holman, as his fighters surged forward.

There are no do-overs in combat. Once you set men and machines in motion, you're committed. You can adjust and maneuver all you want, but if you start off with a blunder, the odds are, things will only get worse.

A key factor in all battles is attack position. The tactical egg displayed on Holman's radar scope, showed the effects of his maneuvering. The turning radius of a space dogfight can be executed in an infinite number of geometric volumes. It allowed the pilot to turn at high power thrusts.

A Titan ship blipped onto Holman's screen and then disappeared. He only caught a glimpse, but it was enough to lay in an intercept course.

He shoved his stick hard over. His Viper grumbled as it accelerated. He felt the adrenaline rush of the crushing speed.

His target had a considerable lead, but the Viper's powerful engines would apply all the acceleration he needed to close the gap.

A cluster of enemy ships loomed ahead. He straightened up and turned to avoid several of them. He maneuvered through a series of extended S-shape. Glen Holman shifted into a turn.

Another glimpse of the target told him, he was closing in.

He aimed his ship on an intercept to the Titan. As he led the group toward the Titans' flank, he snapped out orders to assign targets.

A minute later, he ordered, "Fire missiles!"

The Titans responded with decoys and electronic jamming. But the missiles were effective against the formation.

After a minute, he glanced at his scanner. His target had vanished. He felt a momentary concern, but a moment later, he caught another glimpse.

He swung back and zig-zagged, driving his ship hard.

The target managed to stay ahead of him by tracing a cleaner path.

Glen Holman scolded himself for his shoddy flying.

Keep focused.

Staying in target's track, he closed. He strained on each turn.

Another glimpse told him that the enemy had radically altered course. A moment later, he understood why. Several Titan fighters were coming to the ship's aid.

There are too many.

A touch of fear registered. He aimed his ship's nose away. Over tac 1 he reported, "I have three bandits on my six."

He knew it would take several minutes for his squadron members to respond to the message. By then, it might be all over—one way or another.

The three fighters were on an intercept course with Glen Holman.

He considered the Titan ships, trying to gauge their strengths and weaknesses. Their power profile was not very different from his own.

"We're coming," yelled Bear from flight one.

Glen Holman felt the weight of acceleration as his Viper turned. He maneuvered.

The enemy fighters launched another salvo. The eerie glow of residual explosion gases flashed by. The enemy craft adjusted its attack vector and oriented in a new direction. He pressed his engines to deliver more thrust. His AI screamed a warning that the enemy was acquiring a missile lock at 80% effective.

Every second was an eternity as he watched the lock warning approach 100%. He went into standard evasion protocol releasing jammers and decoys. He put his finger on the weapon's trigger. He fired both forward rail cannons sending ballistic metal at his enemy. He whipped the fighter around in a tight arc as his enemy met a fiery death.

Lorelei Steward adjusted her radar display and armed her weapon systems. She loaded the updated targeting information. Next, she assigned priority targets to her bombers. Her plasma cannon booted up along with the missile-select console.

Lorelei pulled her safety strap tight against the cushioned seat in her Viper II. She hardly had a moment before her ship acceleration drove her into her seat. The inky black surrounded her, sending a tingle along her spine.

Lorelei's rapid mind flew to reconsidering the cold math of the logistics. Missile launches prepared to send waves of destruction to a heavily defended enemy carrier, the *Verspa*.

At first the Titans appeared uncertain how best to respond. Then the CSP accelerated to intercept the bombers. At .3 C light-speed, it would take time to reach them.

Lorelei analyzed the display screens. "That's what I was waiting for. They're at their most vulnerable. It's our best chance. We must fight while they have the fewest fighters to defend themselves."

Her wingman said, "Look at that. The Titans must be boiling mad. They have to attack directly into our overlaying defensive fire."

The greatest gain possible was to keep the formation tight all the way toward the carriers. But Lorelei knew that she had to split the formation into separate attack flights to go after each carrier.

A moment later, Lorelei ordered, "Execute targeting plan. Flight leaders, follow the designated vectors and press your attack home. We have to get those carriers."

The starfighters split into four flights and stuck. The Titans threw up a wall of flak.

Lorelei led flight one, and though she concentrated on precision flying. She dodged incoming missiles, and Titan fighters caused her to miss her timing window. She was forced to shift her position. The flak got heavier. She had to penetrate anti-missiles, jammers, and decoys.

"I got bandits at two o'clock," screamed Flannery.

At 1534, the *Constellation* OOD reported, "Message from the *Yorktown*, sir."

Gallant read:

> From: *Yorktown*
> To: *Constellation*
>> The situation is now very grave.
>> Titan cruiser destroyer squadron is bombarding Mars.
>> Enemy space wing is smashing through Earth's defenses.
>> We are suffering unsustainable losses.
>> Imperative you prevent further starfighters waves, or we shall perish.
>> *Admiral George Collingsworth*

Before Gallant could react to the information, the OOD said, "Enemy dreadnaughts are approaching, sir. Will we withdraw out of range?"

Gallant's plan of diverting some Titan strength away from Earth to help the convoy had unintended consequences. Vvorn had sent a larger than expected dreadnaught force to his rear and back to the convoy. Gallant was close to their path if they chose to go for him. He was in trouble.

"No. We must close the range to the carriers and send a second wave of starfighters to finish them off."

"But we will come under fire from the dreadnaughts very soon."

"Maintain course."

"Sir, do you wish to redirect our starfighter to strike the dreadnaughts instead of the enemy carriers?"

"No. We must keep attacking those carriers until they are destroyed. We can't fail!"

CHAPTER 25

No Man Left Behind

The *Constellation* came under fire from pursuing Titan dreadnaughts. Titan starfighters swarmed about her, as well. The enemy formation fired their long-range ship-killer missiles while their starfighters swooped in and added their firepower. The Titans wanted to extract their full measure of revenge against the *Constellation* after the destruction she had wrought against their carriers.

Gallant could see no chance for immediate escape. He kept his few CSP fighters close for defense, and his escorts supported him as well as possible. He braced himself for the onslaught that was about to happen.

The flight director vectored out the combat space patrol to cover the more vulnerable quarters of the carrier. He conducted operations to optimize protection. However, the enemy's remaining starfighters attacked in large numbers and quickly overwhelmed the few starfighters Gallant had retained for defense.

"Be prepared for rapid maneuvering," he said to the bridge crew. "I want the ship handled with lightning precision. We won't get any second chances."

The Chief-of-the-watch barked, "Look sharp all of you."

"Which way will they go?" asked the OOD, referring to the pursuing dreadnaughts.

"It doesn't matter which way they turn. We'll go the opposite direction."

The sensor operator said, "Enemy has turned to starboard on an intercepting course."

"Hard to port," ordered Gallant. After a minute, he added, "steady as you go. Keep her there."

He kept his eye on the main viewscreen with an occasional glance at his command console. Status lights blinked green, yellow, and red demanding attention he couldn't afford to show them. He watched the vector arrows on his display screen adjust to the new situation. It was the squadron's task to maintain formation relative to the carrier.

Did I gain distance?

No. Another few seconds told him the enemy was closer.

"Incoming missiles," from a sensor operator.

The *Constellation* came under fire. Initially, the missiles passed wide, but then they achieved greater accuracy as the distance decreased. He ordered the full complement of anti-missile defense, jamming, decoys, and coordinated rail-gun fire.

Gallant was nearly knocked over by the recoil

of the first direct hit.

He observed, "This is getting too hot to last long."

Straightening himself up, he walked into CIC to get a clearer picture of the latest data. When he returned to the bridge, he ordered, "Have the destroyers launch an attack."

The OOD issued the orders.

The cruiser *Cassandra* and *Astoria* led the destroyers in an attacking sortie directly at the dreadnaughts. They hoped to distract the enemy from their demolition of the *Constellation*. No one could guess if their plan would work, but they bravely went forth.

The appearance of this small assault caused a momentary hesitation on the Titans part, but they merely shifted their secondary batteries to deal with *Cassandra's* troop. The small force was quickly dispatched. Then the dreadnaughts resumed concentrated fire at the *Constellation*.

He ordered, "Hard to starboard." A minute later, he ordered, "Hard to port." Gallant twisted and turned the ship to try and throw off the enemy guidance systems.

He released jamming gear and decoys and drones, everything he could throw out was sent to interfere with the enemy's target acquisition process.

"All weapons stations, pour it on. Give them everything you've got."

The ship's systems erupted with missiles, lasers, and rail guns, but their caliber couldn't match the oversized dreadnaught weapons.

The *Constellation's* starfighters concentrated their missiles on the lead dreadnaught. Their missiles were hitting home, and that ship was staggered. But there were more ships. The dreadnaughts were supremely powerful and unrelenting. Without mercy, they continued to pour on their hateful rath.

Gallant scanned the latest communication messages. No one was coming to his aid. There were no additional ships he could call on. Everyone was too far away.

At first, the shields of the *Constellation* held as missile after missiles exploded against it. They came alive glowing as they repelled blasts, lasers, plasma, and rail gun shells. The hull shield heated crackled and turned bright red. Enormous unimaginable power surged around them. The rail guns roared, and shells torn at the enemy.

Fire bathed the black of space in a brilliant spectrum of light.

"What the hell?"

Distant explosions erupted.

This was a nightmare from which he couldn't wake himself. The might weapons fired. Cannisters of metal flew toward them.

A jet of plasma hit the ship.

The ship shook.

Alarms rang out. Smoke filled the bridge and the call for the damage control teams was sounded.

"Shields holding, sir." The nuclear blasts were dispersed and left behind as the carrier accelerated away.

But soon, the deluge of nuclear blasts, plasma smashes, laser splatter, and railgun impacts took a toll that no ship could resist. Its rate of fire was slacking. More and more weapons systems were damaged and off-line. More and more crewmen were killed and not replaced. The hanger deck was set ablaze. No more flight operations were possible.

Their latest antagonist closed the range and sent a missile directly at the ships aft section. A major explosion rocked the engineering spaces and left a huge whole in the side of the carrier. Propulsion was lost. Another dreadnaught approached the stern of the crippled ship.

Gallant looked at the display console in complete helplessness.

The *Constellation* was breaking apart and becoming a shadow of its former self. Another explosion occurred and shrapnel killed the chief, nearly cutting him in two.

Gallant balanced in his mind the loss of one carrier against the harm she had inflicted on Vvorn's fleet. She had accounted for three enemy carriers and a dreadnaught as well as numerous escorts and starfighters. He knew, however, that the personal loss was greater. He would wrestle with the mental unease that it was his decisions that had brought him and thousands of his shipmates to this end. He wasted another few seconds in gloomy self-reflection.

It seemed then that the din redoubled. Around him were the slaughtered bodies of many crewmen. The deck was littered with the dead even as others were hacking away broken pipes and clearing wreckage in a hopeless effort to return systems to service.

Wordlessly, Gallant watched as his pride and joy was rendered into a derelict.

I've failed.

In past battles, time seemed to slow down. Now it seemed to whiz bye, giving him no chance to consider all that remained to be done—he had to save his crew.

If this were a conventional war, he would surrender. He would lower his colors and accept internment. But the Titans didn't take prisoners.

He ordered, "Abandon ship! Abandon ship."

Gallant was manic as he ordered shuttles and small craft to be filled with crewmembers and wounded. Figures hurried about in the smoke. The moved through the damaged areas as air hissed out of small hull holes. The enemy's attention shifted to the other squadron ships, giving the *Constellation's* survivors hope for later rescue. One after another, the little craft launched and scattered away.

Aboard the *Constellation,* things were going from bad to disastrous. Gallant directed the medical responders to help the needy getaway.

How much time do I have?

Until what? Will the entire ship implode?!

After an unendurable period, everyone they could find alive was gone. The final shuttle waited for him, but he wasn't willing to leave just yet. He ran through the compartments to ensure there would be no one left behind. To his dismay, he found several badly wounded sailors on the engineering deck. Those who had arrived to remove them were themselves hurt from exploding shrapnel.

Gallant called for another rescue team from the shuttle to take them aboard. But now, the shuttle was overfull. He directed them to depart.

"Sir, what about you?"

"I'll take an escape pod." He ordered, "Go! Go!"

Reluctantly, the shuttle pilot left.

"Where the hell is an escape pod?" he shouted into his AI comm pin.

The AI replied, "One hundred meters along the next corridor."

Gallant ran with his heart pounding. He listened to his steps echo behind him. Everything else was silent.

He hoped to reach the escape pod, but hope was a fragile thing.

The atmosphere was slowly bleeding off from the many hull punctures. The electrical panels crackled and sparked. Twisted metal structures distorted the memory of his ship.

Heat and humidity formed beads of sweat that rolled over down his forehead as his battle armor attempted to meet his respiratory needs.

The ship's oxygen generators, CO_2 scrubbers, and electric generators were almost completed destroyed or inoperable. Zipped and buttoned into his battle armor, he had to rely on the pressure suit's air.

Smoke billowed from the AC vents.

Damn environmental system.

An explosion of a nearby electrical panel triggered an even bigger explosion in a hydraulic tank. It sent jagged shrapnel at him hitting him in the shoulder and leg. His armor stopped much, but not all, of the steel. It did, however, save his life.

He opened his eyes to see the compartment a shamble. Laying still on the deck, he listened to the ship's groaning agony synchronize with his own. The drumbeat of the banging metal matched the rhythm of his heart, throb, throb, throb. He feared it would never stop. He tried to yell at the recurring Bang! Bang! Bang! The loud, regular beating throbbed in his ears and drowned out his thoughts.

It continued until he recognized someone was yelling. But he was awash in Bang! Throb! Bang! Throb!

It took several more minutes before he remembered where he was and what was going on.

I've got to make it to the escape pod.

He started.

Where is it?

His hemorrhaging leg made even standing impossible.

He crawled through the deck until he reached an exit point aft of the compartment.

"I can't breathe!"

With his pressure suit ripped he had to rely on the ship's remaining thin atmosphere for air.

"How much oxygen is left?" he asked, expecting an AI reply. But it too was no longer functioning.

His lungs strained to inhale the last of the thin

air. He only drew in an empty breath.

He clenched his hand and crawled. His hollow lungs ached.

Whining machinery died away, and the last glow of emergency lights gasped out.

Lying on his back in pitch black, he wondered if he could go on. The compartment hatches were indistinguishable in the dimness.

Unable to go farther, he sat dripping blood and trembling as the potent grip of shock grabbed hold.

He wanted to yell, "Help." But he had no breath. He thought he heard calling far off.

Hope abandoned him. He needed medical treatment. As his face blanched, he trembled with dizziness, his tunnel vision narrowed, and the room spun.

Closing his eyes, he fought against the pain. He dug his fingernails into his palms to escape the deadness that gnawed inside him. Dark, destructive thoughts flooded in. The future that was supposed to augur success had turned into a nightmare.

His strength gave out.

I'm done.

Then a tiny voice cried out.

"Help!"

Who was that? There wasn't supposed to be anyone left.

"Help!"

There it was again. A woman was crying in pain just a dozen meters away.

She mumbled, "I can't breathe. Help me.

Please!"

Gallant couldn't quit now. Someone needed him. He called upon the last of his willpower and crawled. Fumbling awkwardly, he managed to put a tourniquet on her bleeding arm.

Then together they hobbled along the corridor to a hatch. He couldn't make out the markings in the dark. Straining his fingers, he tried to open it.

No.

He tried the next pod.

No.

Then another.

The hatch to this escape pod opened.

Yes. Finally.

He forced his way into the tiny vehicle and brought the wounded woman with him.

The chamber was claustrophobic. He pressed to release mechanism to eject the pod from the ship.

Nothing happened!

He pressed again and again until he passed out.

CHAPTER 26

Checkmate

A week later, Gallant woke in the Melbourne military hospital. Lying in the regeneration chamber, he heard the buzz of activity around him. There was a good deal of chatter about medicines and vital signs. Oxygen conduits, blood tubes, and electrical wires penetrated his body, allowing chemicals and nano-bots to be pumped throughout his system. Several of his internal organs had been ruptured and had been reconstructed. It took many hours of surgery to cut away dead tissue, perform skin grafts, and inject nano-bots for the final microsurgery. The effort had kept him alive. He was weak as a kitten but eager to get up even though he was sewn together like a rag doll, and every motion was painful.

He fidgeted, trying to find a comfortable position, but to no avail.

The room became quiet when Admiral Collingsworth entered.

The admiral chuckled.

"I beg your pardon, sir, but am I an object of humor?" asked Gallant petulantly as he shifted his position in the regeneration chamber.

"There's nothing at all to laugh about. But there is much to be joyous about. I take it you've heard the news of our victory. Though the *Constellation* was lost, *Glorious* and *Yorktown* swooped in to finish the destruction of the Titan fleet."

"Your victory, sir. You defeated Vvorn's fleet and drove him from the system."

"Yes. I cleaned up the remains. But it was your plan that succeeded. And if you hadn't sacrificed your own ship to stop those carriers . . . well, things could have turned out quite differently.

"But they didn't."

"No. They didn't. They turned out for the better."

A doctor entered. He examined Gallant with a critical eye.

"I'm sure you've seen worse than me?" queried Gallant.

"Actually, no," said the doctor shaking his head. "You and your escape pod companion are on the mend now, but the betting odds were heavily against you both. It was lucky your shipmates went back for you. But I guess I'm something of a magician to salvage what they brought me."

Gallant tried to laugh but ended by let releasing a string of invectives, "Dammit!"

"I'll give you something for that pain," said the

doctor, "but your temper could use some discipline."

Collingsworth chuckled.

Gallant attempted a grin but only produced a grimace. He couldn't wait to get home.

CHAPTER 27

Avalanche

Earth was still celebrating the victory over the Titans when the February weather turned cold and blustery. The air rang with the enthusiastic shouts of glee as the inhabitants breathed a sigh of relief from war. They even frolicked in the massive mountains of snow that descended. But in a shocking political reversal, President Gerome Neumann's genetic laws were repealed by Congress thanks to the grassroots campaign by Alaina Gallant and Edith Collingsworth.

Even though Gallant was still recovering from his wounds, he had been able to serve as a heroic symbol for the popular movement. Which, of course, left President Neumann seriously disgruntled.

So, it was no surprise that when they next met, some volatile words would be exchanged. That opportunity occurred during a military award ceremony with flowery speeches. After the medals' presentation, Neumann stepped away from his entourage and approached Gallant and Alaina backstage. He acknowledged Gallant's salute with a curt nod and ignored Alaina completely.

Keeping his public mask of sincerity on his face, he said, "You two are nothing but trouble."

Gallant exchanged a smile with his wife.

"Gallant, you are an exuberant man. When I first met you, you were full of promise, but you became ensnared in troubles of your own making. You were always trying to prove that you were better than everyone else. These last few months, you and your wife have run wild, out of control."

"We were following our conscience," said Alaina.

Neumann's voice grew louder and more belligerent. "You two think your success gives you the right for impertinence?"

Engrossed in his ire, Neumann stood transfixed for a minute. Finally, he said, "Gallant, your natural abilities have been a source of great frustration to me. You disrupted my agenda to build a thriving society based upon superior genetics. You always had an overinflated ego. Perhaps you still do? Though you should have learned to respect my money and position. They are, after all, the ultimate source of real power."

"Actually, I've learned that there is something more powerful than money or position," said Gallant.

And under the shadow of the snow-covered mountain, Alaina said, "Given the right conditions, even the least voice can start an avalanche."

CHAPTER 28

Superman

The warm spring day was perfect. Alaina stood balanced on a box at the end of a pier. Her loose white cotton blouse and navy skirt let her relish the sun's heat. A mild sunburn colored her exposed arms and legs. She watched as the white-crested waves crashed against the boulders along the shoreline. Where the sky kissed the horizon, a light breeze blew puffy white clouds over a mosaic of red, brown, and green mountains.

She saw him first.

Gallant was some distance away, jostling his way along the beach. He was now fully recovered, and his manly figure captured her imagination. She stood content to merely observe him and carry away the vision. She reflected on her good fortune that they had this joyous day together. She wished she could preserve it in a bottle.

She wondered if the time was right to discuss

their future. Finally, she roused herself and shouted, "Henry? Henry?"

Startled, he raised his head. His eyes brightened immediately, and his lips swelled into a broad smile. He waved back.

"Oh, Henry," she giggled. She laughed so hard she nearly lost her balance and fell off her perch.

A stampede of emotions overwhelmed Alaina, crystallizing into a single thought.

I love him.

In their years together, Alaina had become reconciled to the many privations and disappointments of a navy wife. But she had learned some lessons about her husband that aided their relationship. She had had time to discern the many puzzling behaviors and emotions of the seemingly complex and yet the all too simple man that was Henry Gallant. She understood that the best way to approach him was with a minimum of emotional baggage and a well-thought-out rational argument.

It was one of the things that Gallant claimed he appreciated about her. She got him. She was practical in her approach toward influencing him, and she was usually successful. He respected that. He often said that she knew him better than he knew himself.

They spent a pleasant afternoon on the beach lounging and swimming. They spread a picnic blanket and ate while engaging in light banter. After a while, their conversation turned serious.

She said, "I have always believed that you were special. Your Natural abilities are far superior to anything that the best geneticists have been able to produce. You know it. Julie Ann McCall knows it. George Collingsworth knows it. And even Gerome Neumann knows it."

She touched his arm. "You're a superman, Henry."

Gallant gasped, "Don't use that word. I'm not super. I'm simply different."

But she had made up her mind. "Henry, I want to have a baby. Our baby."

Gallant held his breath.

She said, "I love and admire you, but I am also angry and hurt by you."

Gallant looked away as if seeking escape.

"In a world of genetic engineering, you stand out. And more than that, you are the example that refutes the Titan version of genetic engineering. They picked one person as a universal donor for their entire species. See how that turned out."

He stood motionless.

She continued, "But you are a natural mutation that advances our race, and you must understand that it is more than defending our people today. You must look to the future and let evolution take its course."

"Those are lofty words spoken in broad terms."

Alaina said, "In that case, let's discuss how this concerns us personally."

"I just can't find the words when I think of it in terms of you and me," said Gallant. "I guess I'm a fool."

She stood there a long time as if the strength had left her jaw. She was angry before. Now she was sad.

"Why do you say that?" she asked.

"I said, 'I'm a fool,' because I have no better argument to offer other than an emotional reticence."

She said, "All my life, I've been looking for something. Now I know what it is. I want a child that I can love. I want your child, and I want you to be with me to raise that wonderful new life. I am willing to fight you to make that happen."

Gallant said, "There are legitimate reasons for postponing having a child. There are many threats. It's a great responsibility, for me, for you, and for humanity."

"You are running away from the very thing you should embrace—our hope for the next generation to be better," said Alaina.

He shook his head, "There is no such thing as a superman."

"Some have thought that that might be achieved through genetic engineering. But I believe natural selection has already chosen you to be that being."

She brushed back a lock of brown hair from his forehead and said, "Think of it as just another adventure—a good one."

Alaina watched his resistance melt away.

At long last, Gallant took her into his arms and said, "I'm ready to embrace a new life."

FROM THE AUTHOR

I would be grateful if you could HELP me keep the Henry Gallant series alive by posting a supportive review on the first book of the series, Midshipman Henry Gallant. This will allow me to write more Henry Gallant stories.

Thank you for your kind consideration.
H. Peter Alesso

We are beginning movie development for The Henry Gallant Saga.

Take a look at the book 2 version for the big screen. Now available in preorder for $0.99:

Lieutenant Henry Gallant Screenplay

Can a Natural survive in the 22nd Century genetically engineered space navy?

www.ingramcontent.com/pod-product-compliance
Ingram Content Group UK Ltd.
Pitfield, Milton Keynes, MK11 3LW, UK
UKHW011432040825
7221UKWH00026B/182